SOUTHWEST WISCONSIN LIBRARY SYSTEM
W9-AZG-470

The Million-Dollar Cowboy

This Large Print Book carries the
Seal of Approval of N.A.V.H.

The Million-Dollar Cowboy

MARTHA SHIELDS

Thorndike Press • Thorndike, Maine

Published in 1999 by arrangement with Harlequin Books S.A.

Thorndike Large Print® Americana Series.

The tree indicium is a trademark of Thorndike Press.

The text of this Large Print edition is unabridged.
Other aspects of the book may vary from the original edition.

Set in 16 pt. Plantin.

Printed in the United States on permanent paper.

Library of Congress Cataloging in Publication Data

Shields, Martha.
The million-dollar cowboy / Martha Shields.
p. cm.
ISBN 0-7862-1878-9 (lg. print : hc : alk. paper)
1. Large type books. I. Title.
[PS3569.H4838M5 1999]
813'.54—dc21 99-11203

To Jessica,
my inspiration and my joy.

EDEN
Family Tree

Henry Eden
m. Claire Bristow

Matthew Eden
d. Viet Nam

John Eden
m. Sarah McNeil

1. Hank Eden
m. Alex Miller

3. Travis Eden
m. Becca Larson

2. Claire Eden
m. Jake Anderson

John (J.J.) Eden

Matthew Eden

Sarah Eden

Eden Family Tree Key:

1. Home Is Where Hank Is (SR#1287)
2. And Cowboy Makes Three (SR#1317)
3. The Million-Dollar Cowboy (SR#1346)

Chapter One

National Finals Rodeo
Wednesday, Outside Las Vegas

Travis Eden squinted through the early-afternoon sun as he spotted a column of white smoke. When he crested the next hill he saw the ancient Ford truck spewing it.

His team roping partner and traveling buddy Chance Morgan pointed. "Well, bless my bits. Lookee there, Trav. It's the Ice Queen herself. Who'd'a thought Becca Larson knew how to heat up the engine of a truck? She sure can't heat up a cowboy."

"Becca Larson?" A stampede of conflicting emotions drove through Travis as he eased up on the gas. He'd known Becca since the day she was born — his mother having helped deliver her. For the next eleven years Becca had followed him around like an adoring puppy, until she and her mother were forced off the Circle E when Becca's father died.

Now Becca was the only thing that stood

between Travis and sanity. She once again owned the five hundred acres that Travis had been trying to buy for the past ten years. "What's she doing here?"

"Hell, she's a finalist. Don't you keep up with your profession?"

"Not barrel chasers. Not since . . ." Travis felt his face harden.

Chance chuckled wickedly. "Cheryl-Ann's a finalist, too."

"Good for her," he said tightly and flipped on his turn signal.

"Hey, you ain't gonna stop, are you?"

"Never could pass up a damsel in distress," Travis answered, maneuvering onto the shoulder in front of the disabled truck.

"What do you expect to get out of it? Becca won't give you the time of day, much less thank you. Did you know half the cowboys in the PRCA have had a pool for a year on who could melt the Ice Queen? Not one of us has got so much as a drip off one of her icicles."

Travis pulled up the emergency brake and gave his traveling buddy a hard look. "Hell, Chance, she's just a kid."

"Kid, my horse's butt. She's twenty-six."

"Little Becca's twenty-six?" Travis blinked, then murmured, "I guess she would be, wouldn't she? She was two years behind Claire."

"You know the Ice Queen?"

Travis drew a bead on his team roping partner. Chance Morgan's given name was Brian, but he'd earned the nickname Chance because he'd bet on anything that could run, throw, ride or shoot. He was the best header Travis knew, besides his brother Hank. That's why they were on their way to the National Finals Rodeo. When it came to women, however, Chance had the manners of a polecat. "I know her well enough not to leave a lady stranded in the desert. Didn't your momma teach you any manners?"

Chance snorted. "Hell, Trav. You ain't fun no more."

Travis didn't reply as he switched off the engine. He'd heard that complaint more than once during the past year or so. He'd changed. He knew it as well as Chance. He couldn't pin a date to this transformation, but sometime during the past few years he'd grown tired of the road. Tired of constant pain. Tired of hard landings from flying dismounts off bulls. Tired of a different cheap hotel room every night. Tired of being chased by every buckle bunny in sight. Tired of flashing his "million-dollar smile" for the media, for the sponsors, for all the rodeo fans who wanted an autograph or a picture taken with him. Tired of being — as one ESPN announcer put it — the Michael Jordan of rodeo.

He wanted peace. He wanted out. He wanted to be who he wanted to be, when he wanted to be it. He was determined that this was going to be his last trip to the Finals, his last year on the road.

Travis released a disgusted grunt and swung open the door.

How could that happen when the only place he could find peace — the mountain acres he'd been trying to buy for ten years — had been purchased five months before by the freckle-faced kid he was about to rescue?

Travis's boots hit the asphalt, and he shoved his hat securely down on his head. As long strides took him to the rear of his six-horse trailer, vehicles of all kinds whizzed past on their way into Sin City, aka Las Vegas. He ignored the gusts of cool December wind, but when he cleared the end of the trailer, the sight of a faded pair of blue jeans wrapped around a pair of long legs stopped him dead in his tracks. They began at a pair of scuffed boots resting on the dented bumper of a rusty old Ford truck and rose to a bottom so round and luscious it sent a flash of heat stabbing through his gut.

Shock rendered him immobile. *This* was little Becca Larson? All Travis remembered was a skinny girl with bright copper pigtails and a moonpie face full of freckles.

"Damn."

Travis wasn't aware he'd cussed out loud until Chance came up beside him and said, "Sight's enough to wake the dead, ain't it?"

Aware he was staring, Travis shook off the hottest spell of lust he'd had in a long time and approached the heap of junk a charitable person might call a truck. "Howdy. Need some help?"

"Ow!" As her top half sprang into view, Becca clipped her head on the edge of the hood. A grease-smeared hand flew to her temple and her boots slipped off the bumper.

Always quick on his feet, Travis caught her around the waist to ease her fall. The contours beneath his hands told him her top half had grown up at the same healthy rate as her bottom half.

Heat surged through him like a herd of stampeding cattle. Surprise at the violence of sudden desire made his hands fall away when she twisted in his hold.

Her blue, startled eyes met his and widened even more. "Travis?"

His gaze roamed over the face that had gone from chubby to heart-shaped with a pointed chin and high cheekbones. The copper hair had darkened and deepened until it resembled the deepest coals of a dying fire. The pigtails were now a heavy mass of curls that dragged across slender shoulders. Travis remembered hearing Mrs. Larson complain to his mother about how she'd had to braid Becca's hair when it was wet or she'd never be able to get a comb through it. The ringlets made him want to tug at one, to see how long her hair actually was, to see if it would wrap around his finger like a Christmas ribbon.

"You recognized me?" he asked softly. "I never would've known you in a million years, monkey-face."

Her face softened for a brief instant at the old nickname, transporting him back twenty years to a time when she worshipped him as only a kid can do. He wasn't a rodeo star back then, just a mixed-up kid himself who basked in her adoration like plants bask in sunshine. He'd forgotten how good that felt.

Suddenly her eyes narrowed and she stepped back, breaking the light hold of his arms. "Of course I recognize you. Every person who's ever seen a Wrangler blue jeans ad knows what you look like. And your picture is plastered all over every issue of the *Prorodeo Sports News*."

Travis frowned. So she saw him as the Million-Dollar Cowboy with the Million-Dollar Smile. Just like everybody else. Somehow he'd hoped —

What? That he'd finally found a woman who knew the real Travis Eden? Who might actually want Travis Eden the man, not the star? Fat chance. He'd learned the hard way that wasn't going to happen.

Swallowing disappointment that was somehow more bitter than usual, Travis pushed his hat back on his head and flashed the smile that had helped make him famous. "Sorry about your head. We didn't mean to sneak up on you. Just stopped to see if we could help out."

Becca sent a glance from his hat to his boots, then did the same to Chance. When the eyes that were as clear as crystals came back to his, Travis had the distinct impression she didn't approve of what she'd seen.

"We're fine." Turning, she placed one boot on the bumper.

Travis blinked at her cool dismissal. His smile faded. "Fine, hell. You're spewing like Old Faithful."

"Tell me something I don't know." She lifted herself onto the bumper easily. "It's nothing I can't handle."

Chance touched his sleeve. "Come on, Trav. Told you she wouldn't want our help."

Travis yanked his arm away. "I can't just —"

"Howdy, boys. Thanks for stopping by."

"Mrs. Larson?" Travis turned as Becca's mother came around the truck. He was as shocked by the changes in her as he'd been by those in her daughter. The last fifteen years had not been kind to Joy Larson.

Several inches shorter than Becca, Mrs. Larson had the same ice blue eyes and the same trim figure as her daughter, but there the similarities ended. Mrs. Larson's hair was pale blond, lightened even further now with streaks of white. A web of fine wrinkles around her eyes and lips gave her a pinched expression — as if she dealt with constant pain.

Travis didn't know whether that pain was physical or emotional, and the sudden determination to find out twisted his gut. He didn't want to feel sorry for the Larsons. They'd stolen his future when they purchased their old ranch, the Circle E.

But his resentment warred with guilt. Mrs. Larson had given him so much when he was growing up. She and Becca had been there for him during those terrible years after his parents died, when he'd needed someone to believe in him.

Mrs. Larson smiled weakly. "Travis Eden, are you too big a star to give your old friend a hug?"

The guilt stabbed deep as Travis stepped forward and wrapped the frail body in a tight embrace. The last time he'd hugged this woman was the day her ranch had been sold at auction, six months after her husband died and left her burdened with debts. He was just seventeen and helpless to help the small family who'd become as close to him as his own. They'd moved away, and a year later he'd turned professional bull rider. He kept meaning to track them down, but the years slipped by one by one until the Larsons had faded to a distant memory.

"It's good to see you again." Mrs. Larson patted him as he released her, then she turned to Chance. "I don't believe I've had the pleasure . . ."

"This is Chance Morgan," Travis told her as Chance nodded. "He's been my team roping partner most of this year."

"You qualified for the Finals in team roping, Travis?" she asked.

"Yes, ma'am."

"You're usually here for bull riding, aren't you?"

Travis felt lower than a worm's belly. Apparently the Larsons had kept up with him over the years. At the same time he was warmed by the knowledge that they'd cared enough to follow his career. "Yes, ma'am. I'm here for that, too."

"Did you hear that, Becca? Travis qualified in two events."

"I know, Momma," Becca mumbled from the depths of the engine.

"My, you've had a busy year. I'd ask about your family, but I've probably seen them since you have. Did you know we're neighbors again?"

"Yes, ma'am." Travis couldn't help asking, "How'd you get old man Duggan to let go of the Circle E?"

"Why, he seemed happy to get rid of it," Mrs. Larson replied. "All we did was ask."

Travis's face tightened. Figured. Though Travis had made countless offers to Duggan over the past ten years, the old man had refused to sell him a single stick on the property. Duggan blamed Travis for his son's death during a high school rodeo.

Said Travis should've talked Ray out of riding the bronc he'd drawn. Duggan probably laughed with glee as he signed over the deed.

Mrs. Larson pulled her sweater closer against the chilly December breeze. "Well, thank goodness you stopped. I've been telling Becca for weeks we should —"

"They don't want to hear our troubles, Momma," Becca cut in, throwing an irritated look over her shoulder.

Mrs. Larson's hands fluttered up and down in a gesture Travis remembered well. It still reminded him of a butterfly. "I don't know anything about motor engines, but I do believe this one's on its last leg. We've put so many miles on it, it's lost count. I just don't know what we're going to do."

Becca twisted around. "We're going to let these cowboys be on their way, aren't we, Momma?" she said in a voice dripping with sugar.

"But, dear, Travis went to all the trouble to stop. The least you could do is let him look at the engine."

Becca hopped off the bumper to place her hands on her hips. "Why? Because he's a rodeo cowboy? And who better to look at an engine than someone who spends his life on the road? Well, you may be right there, but nobody knows this engine better than me. I've been fixing it for the last eight years. I can fix it today."

Travis lifted a brow at her sarcasm. "Doesn't look like you've had much success so far."

"It just needs a chance to cool down."

"Come on, Travis, let's go."

Travis ignored Chance's suggestion. Brushing past Becca, he tossed his hat on the windshield and stuck his head under the hood. He felt the truck dip slightly as Becca joined him.

"I can handle this, Travis," she insisted. "I'm not a little girl anymore."

His eyes lifted and locked into hers. "Yeah, I noticed."

She caught a quick breath, making her nostrils flare the tiniest bit, making Travis want to drag her across the hot engine into his arms. Startled by the intensity of the feeling, he tore his gaze from hers and asked, "Since the smoke's white, it's got to be the radiator. Right?"

"Yes, but it's just a little hole," she insisted, fanning trails of steam out of the way. "See? It's about cooled down enough to plug it up."

He leaned farther over to peer down at

the radiator. "Little hole? Hell, that thing's as big as Texas."

"No, it's not." She fanned furiously and leaned farther in. "It's . . . Dang. It is big, isn't it? I couldn't see earlier because of the steam . . ."

Hearing despair in her voice, Travis glanced up to see tears of frustration turning her eyes to crystal as she stared down at the busted radiator. She blinked them away rapidly.

"I doubt you've a drop of water or antifreeze left," he said gently. "Good thing we stopped."

Their eyes met over the engine. Travis could read the obvious doubt in hers as she returned his steady gaze. There was a slash of grease smeared across her cheek that his fingers ached to wipe away. Would her flushed skin feel as hot as it looked? Would he be able to feel her pulse under the —

"Thank you. I guess we do need your help," she said finally, yanking his wandering mind back to reality. She sighed heavily and muttered, "Looks like some things never change."

Travis smiled, glad to know she remembered all the times he'd chopped wood for their stove or played hooky from school to drive their small herd to spring pasture or stopped by with a haunch of beef. Confused as much by the sudden feeling of tenderness as he'd been by his unexpected surge of desire, he straightened and clipped the back of his head on the hood. "Ow!"

Hearing a soft laugh, he glared at Becca as he rubbed his head. But the sight of her wide smile poking dimples in cheeks sprinkled with freckles made him forget the pain, nearly made him forget his name.

She covered her impish grin with slender fingers. "Sorry."

"No, you're not, monkey-face." With a smile, he grabbed his hat and grimaced as he settled it on his head. "We'll give you and your mother a ride into Las Vegas, then you can —"

The grin vanished. "Whoa! Back up the trailer. Las Vegas is sixty miles away."

Travis looked at Chance, then at Mrs. Larson, then back to Becca. "Give or take a few. That's where you're heading, isn't it?"

She hopped down from the bumper. "Well, of course. But I can't leave my truck sitting here that long. I've got a horse in that rig."

Travis pointed to his own. "And I've got

four horses in a six-horse trailer. Plenty of room for yours."

Her chin lifted. "But —"

"You've got two choices," he said, deliberately cutting her off. "We can head on into Las Vegas and find some place willing to come this far to haul your rig back."

Her thin red brows nearly touched. "How much would that cost?"

Travis glanced at Chance. "What? At least a hundred, I'd say. Wouldn't you?"

"This far?" Chance shook his head. "Closer to two hundred."

Becca gasped. "Two hundred dollars just to get it there? And then pay to fix it? I don't like that option. What's the other?"

"There's an ex-rodeo cowboy in Glendale. He owns the gas station about ten miles down the road. Name's Rube Pruitt. He's a good man and a good mechanic. He can fix your truck for a fair price."

"Today?"

Travis shrugged. "Probably not, but you can ask."

"I have to be at the welcoming reception tonight," Becca said. "It's required."

"Yep," Travis agreed. "We all have to go."

"But I can't just leave my truck in Glendale. That's fifty miles from Las Vegas.

How will I get to the arena? And where will we sleep?"

Her question surprised him. "What do you mean, where will you sleep?"

She pointed to the camper on the back of her truck. "We've got a space reserved at a campground on the Boulder highway."

"Campground? Do you know how cold the desert gets at night in December?"

"We always camp," Mrs. Larson said. "We're used to it."

"Well, tonight you'll have to stay at a hotel." Travis turned toward the beat-up double horse trailer at the back of the beat-up truck. "If you can find one with a room. Vegas during Finals is as full as a summer tick, and I heard they have several other large conventions in town this week."

Becca followed him every step. "And if we can't find a room?"

He shrugged. "We'll cross that stream when we come to it. Chance? Instead of just standing around looking like a moose froze on its feet, go open up my trailer."

"Can we afford a room in a hotel, Becca?" Mrs. Larson asked.

"Of course not, Momma."

At the back of the horse trailer, Travis spun around. "What do you mean you can't afford it? You're one of the world's top-fifteen money winners in barrel racing or you wouldn't be here."

"That doesn't mean we're made of money," Becca insisted. "I'm not a seven-time world champion bull rider with endorsement patches all over my rig. Besides, I have to save every dollar if I'm going to —"

"To what?" he demanded when she cut herself off with a guilty look.

She regarded him steadily, her eyes full of distrust. "Never mind."

"You mean if you're going to pay for a busted radiator?" he snapped at her, irritated that she didn't trust him.

His words shook the loop out of her lasso. When she looked away, deflated, Travis wanted to draw her into his arms and comfort her. Startled by the powerful impulse, he reached for the latch on the trailer door to keep from reaching for her.

He tried to tell himself the feeling was a remnant of the brotherly affection he'd had for her years ago, but didn't believe it for a minute. He wasn't Becca's brother and — though his mind told him he was a damn fool — at the moment he was very, very glad.

"Get a hold of yourself," he murmured.

"What?"

He shook away his wandering thoughts. This was Becca Larson, damn it. The woman who'd stolen his ranch. "The hotels are offering special rates to finalists. It won't break you."

"That's what you think," she mumbled.

"What did you say?"

She bent to catch a grain bag that had settled against the door of the trailer. "Nothing."

Travis had another sudden urge — to grab her and make her talk to him. To demand to know why she'd bought the Circle E when she still had years left to make her mark in barrel racing. To demand she sell it to him.

He didn't grab her, but the idea played through his mind as he hauled down the ramp and released the butt chain.

Why not spend time with the Larsons and see if he couldn't talk them into selling him the Circle E? Becca had only been barrel racing for a little over a year, according to his brother Hank. She was just beginning her rodeo career. She'd be on the road, away from the home she'd just redeemed. She didn't need the burden of maintaining a ranch, too. Hell, chances were she'd find some cowboy to settle down with along the way and wind up selling the Circle E anyway. He could just persuade her to do it sooner rather than later.

Since this was the Larsons' first trip to Vegas, he could show them the town, help them when they needed help, be the escort ladies needed in Sin City. Who better than an old friend? He had ten days to turn on the charm, to convince them he needed the five hundred acres that lay along the northwest border of his family ranch more than they did.

Travis hesitated, remembering how his libido had been doing a damn fine imitation of a Ping-Pong ball ever since he'd stopped. The last thing he needed was to get involved with Becca. He had to spend time alone on Yellow Jack Mountain before he could think about sharing his life — and he had a feeling that with this woman it would be all or nothing.

On the other hand, in order to spend time on Yellow Jack Mountain he had to have the Circle E, which meant he needed to convince the Larsons to sell it to him.

He'd just have to watch himself around Becca. So what if he responded to her more than he had to any woman in years? It was probably just the shock of seeing her all grown-up. He'd be okay if he kept reminding himself she was only little monkey-face.

Smiling at his plan, Travis stepped into the two-horse trailer. Though the heavy steel rig looked beat-up on the outside, inside the trailer was immaculate. The liver chestnut stood on the left side of the center partition. Hay, two saddles and tack took up the other side. The mare was protected with a head guard, wrapped legs and tail, plus a blanket for good measure. The wooden floor looked new and the rubber mats on top were swept clean.

Hank always said you could tell a lot about a person by the way they treat their animals. Travis's estimation of Becca rose. She might be tight when it came to her own comfort, but she made sure her horse had a safe, clean ride.

"What's wrong?" she asked anxiously.

"Not a thing." He stepped to the front of the trailer and unhooked the mare, talking soothingly as he urged her back down the ramp.

Becca reached for the bridle as soon as the horse cleared the trailer, but Travis shook his head. "She's a bit skittish because of the traffic. I'll get her in my trailer. You get your clothes and things. One way or another, you don't have much choice but to ride into Vegas with me."

Becca reluctantly let go of the bridle, but stroked her hand lovingly down the mare's neck. "Momma's packing our things."

"Best bring your saddles and anything else of value, then," he said as he led the mare down the lee side of the rig.

"You have room for all this and four people, too?"

Travis glanced back over his shoulder and grinned. "If not, we'll put you in back with the livestock."

Becca shifted closer to the left, trying to avoid Chance as he stretched his legs out in the cramped space they shared in the back of the extended cab. Not that she could blame him. She was a good six inches shorter, and she felt like a sardine.

" 'Scuse me," Chance murmured.

Becca nodded and turned her attention to the scenery out the window. She was being rude to the cowboy who'd given up his front seat to her mother, but she couldn't help it. She didn't like Chance Morgan, not since he tried to corner her behind the chutes last winter in Toledo. She'd broken away from him then, but now she felt him watching her, and it reminded her of that day all over again.

To escape, Becca closed her eyes and leaned her head against the window. She didn't know whether to laugh or cry. Who would've thought she'd be riding into Las Vegas behind the most famous cowboy in rodeo?

She knew Travis would be at the Finals, but she thought he'd ignore her like he'd done over the last year at the few rodeos where they were both entered. She'd tried to make an effort to speak to him the first couple of times — mostly because her mother insisted — but he was constantly surrounded by people. Though he always smiled, somehow she'd known he wasn't enjoying himself, and she didn't want to annoy him further. After that she figured he'd forgotten who she was, that he'd become too big a star to recognize a stupid kid who grew up worshipping him.

Now she didn't know what to think. Thank heaven there wasn't any danger of her slipping back into that same old role.

Travis's deep, rumbling voice asked her mother a question, drawing Becca's eyes open and to his profile. A shiver of awareness tingled over every nerve ending in her body.

Except it wouldn't be the same role. The adoration she'd had for him as a child never felt like this. His smile had never made her feel as if she'd suddenly been dropped into a hot tub. His voice wasn't as deep then, didn't send echoes of heat sinking into her muscles, making them suddenly weak. His touch hadn't made her feel as if she'd poked her finger into an electrical outlet.

Why did she have to run into Travis now? This way? If she'd come across him during one of the rodeo events, she could've simply said, "Hello. How are you? Nice to see you." And that would've been that.

This reminded her too much of the charity case she and her mother had been when they lived on the Circle E years ago. Not that Becca had been aware of it then. It wasn't until she was older that she'd realized how much the Edens had helped them. First Mrs. Eden came with Travis and Claire in tow. Then Travis had continued coming after his parents died, often bringing Claire to play with Becca.

Becca had spent the past ten years working hard so she'd never be a charity case again. It rankled to be put in that position again. And somehow it rankled even more for Travis to see her as one — again.

Her truck couldn't have picked a worse time to break down. This wasn't any ordinary rodeo they were headed to where the most she could lose was a night's purse and an entry fee. It was the National Finals. If she missed one of the ten nights — for any reason — she could kiss the championship goodbye.

Becca couldn't stop her hands from curling into fists. She had to win that championship. If she didn't, she'd lose the Circle E just like they'd lost it fifteen years ago when her father died. She needed every penny of that money to pay off the loan Ote Duggan had called in after his uncle died two months ago.

Now she had to spend no telling how much of her hard-earned money not only on repairs to her truck, but on a hotel room and other expenses — meals and tips and who knew what else? Camping was so much cheaper. Space cost ten dollars a night instead of fifty to a hundred, and they could cook their own meals.

Over the smooth rumble of the truck Becca heard her mother's voice talking quietly to Travis about moving back to Wyoming. Having the family ranch back meant so much to her mother. Joy Larson had been born on the Circle E. And now she was going to die there.

Tears sprang to Becca's eyes like they did every time she thought about the tumor in her mother's brain that was slowly killing her. Inoperable, the doctors said.

"Don't worry about your truck. Rube Pruitt will take good care of it," a deep voice said from the front seat, startling Becca out of her thoughts.

She glanced up and met Travis's shaded blue eyes in the rearview mirror. She could only see part of his face in the narrow glass, but she knew his features. He had so many endorsement contracts his All-American smile flashed from the pages of every rodeo and Western magazine published. Women all over the United States — probably the world — swooned over the square jaw, the broken nose, the high cheekbones and broad forehead that were so chiseled he looked like the first draft of some cowboy sculpture.

Becca's chin lifted. But not her. She didn't have time for hero worship at this point in her life — especially not for a rodeo cowboy. "I'd never heard of Rube Pruitt before today."

"I know him well," Travis answered, shifting his eyes back to the road. "He's a good man. Rode saddle broncs back when Hank first turned pro."

"Well, he might be trustworthy, but I don't like being fifty miles away from my truck."

Becca saw his shoulder raise and lower. "It was your choice. You could've gotten a tow from Las Vegas."

"I know. But I can't afford to pay two hundred dollars for a tow on top of what it's going to cost to fix the radiator." She heaved a sigh. "And who knows how many crooked mechanics there are in a town like Vegas."

His eyes found hers again, his grin wide and knowing. "You mean you're trusting *my* judgment?"

Becca tore her gaze away, barely restraining herself from sticking out her tongue at him like she used to do when he teased her. The trouble was, deep down she did trust him — and that scared her more than the thought of coming in dead last in the Finals.

Travis Eden was the ideal rodeo cowboy, but over the years Becca had learned that rodeo cowboys weren't worth spitting on if they caught on fire. They stole your heart, then they blithely went on down the road. From her saddle bronc riding father to the sweet-talking stable hand turned bull rider she'd almost given her heart to back in Paris, Texas, they were all the same. Love 'em and leave 'em was their credo — with emphasis on leaving.

Becca didn't want anything to do with Travis Eden or any other rodeo cowboy. Maybe she'd had a crush on him years ago, but that was before she knew the inner workings of a rodeo cowboy's mind — what limited workings there were.

If she trusted him now, it was only about truck repairs and only because she had no other choice.

With a sigh, she rubbed the tense spot between her eyebrows. It had been a long day. She'd be glad when they reached Las Vegas. The hotel would be worth every penny if she never had to lay eyes on Travis Eden again.

Chapter Two

Wednesday, Diamond Spurs Hotel and Casino

"Oh, my!" Mrs. Larson breathed as they entered the lobby of the hotel. "Oh, my, my, my."

"Momma, hush," Becca said under her breath. "You haven't said anything but 'Oh, my' since we left the arena." Travis had stopped first at the Thomas and Mack Center where the Finals were held to check their horses into the temporary stalls set up for the finalists. "People will think you've never been in a hotel before."

"But I haven't," her mother uttered unapologetically. "Not like this."

The lobby of the Diamond Spurs Hotel and Casino put the word "plush" to shame. Thick, brightly patterned carpet rolled beneath their feet as they wound their way around countless rows of slot machines and gaming tables. Crystal chandeliers did little to light the dim interior, but were breathtaking if you could glance up from the melee of gamblers long enough to enjoy them. Women in skimpy saloon-girl costumes carried drinks to cowboys, cowgirls and patrons of all nationalities. The noise of the slot machines, standing like rows of one-armed thieves, was deafening.

Becca knew she wouldn't be feeding those greedy bandits. Dropping money into a machine just to watch fruit and bars spin was not her idea of a good time. But as she pushed through the casino on the way to the hotel desk, she nodded to someone who was doing exactly that — CherylAnn Barnes, a barrel-racing finalist from Oklahoma. Her main competition.

CherylAnn returned her cool nod, then the bleached blonde's brown eyes lit up when they looked past her. "Travis!" she cried, shoving Becca's mother aside in her rush to get at him. "You finally made it!"

Becca caught her mother, then turned to glare at CherylAnn. The blonde wrapped her arms around Travis's neck and planted her lips on his.

Travis didn't look pleased at the attack and used his free hand in a vain attempt to extract himself, which surprised Becca. She knew — from CherylAnn's bragging at various rodeos — that Travis and CherylAnn had been engaged a couple of years ago. According to CherylAnn, she was the one who broke things off two months before the wedding, that she'd broken Travis's heart. She claimed all she had to do was snap her quirt, and Travis would once again be kissing her boots.

Hearing about their engagement had been the point where Becca had stopped trying to get Travis's attention. Anyone who could fall in love with that selfish, spoiled, Daddy's girl wasn't someone Becca wanted to know.

As she watched them, however, Becca's heart took a diving leap for her stomach. Disgust. That's all it was. Still, it took an effort to wrench her eyes away from the long, hot kiss CherylAnn pressed on Travis. "Come on, Momma. Let's go get a room."

Becca paused at the end of the check-in desk where a life-size cutout of Travis stood with the words Special Appearances by the Diamond Spurs Million-Dollar Cowboy with the Million-Dollar Smile — Travis Eden blazoned across his broad chest. The sign went on to give the dates and times.

"Enjoying the view?" Travis's deep voice

rumbled close to her ear, causing shivers to race across her skin.

"Hardly." Tamping down her reaction with a reminder of whose hands had just been crawling all over him, Becca swiveled her head. She frowned when she saw he was alone. "Where's CherylAnn? Looked like you two would be reliving old times for hours."

For an instant Travis lost his Million-Dollar Smile. "Hardly."

If she hadn't been watching his face, she would've missed the brief lapse. Before she could comment, his smile snapped back into place.

With a hand on the small of her back, he gave a gentle push toward the check-in counter. "The line's not getting any shorter, monkey-face."

Puzzled at his reaction, Becca moved to stand behind her mother, who'd gone ahead. A moment later Chance came up behind them.

"What's CherylAnn doing here?" Travis asked. "I didn't want to stick around long enough to find out. Aren't barrel racers at another hotel?"

"The Las Vegas Club." Chance patted his shirt pocket. "Got her number. You don't mind if I give her a try, do you?"

"Hell, join the crowd," Travis mumbled.

"That CherylAnn's quite a little number, ain't she?" Chance said in a low, lecherous tone.

Travis's voice tightened. "I don't know."

"Hellfire, you two was engaged." Chance lowered his voice. "And I heard that a couple of years ago in Salinas, you two went up under the bleachers and —"

"Shut up, Chance," Travis said irritably. "You hear too damn much. And you talk too damn much, too."

"Ah, hell, Trav. You ain't no —"

"Yeah, yeah. I'm no fun anymore. I heard you before."

"Yeah, well, you ain't."

At that point, a couple of teenage girls in tight jeans and boots came up and asked Travis for his autograph. As he obliged, Becca breathed a silent prayer of thanks as the cowboys were forced to shut up. She'd heard more than enough about CherylAnn Barnes.

Several minutes later, however, she prayed they would start talking again — on any subject. Finished with the adolescent fawning session, Travis stood in line right behind her. She was acutely aware of every breath he took, every time he shifted his duffel bag from one hand to the other. Several times he accidentally brushed against her back, and she felt heat sliding all the way down to her toes.

With sudden shock, she realized her reactions had all the earmarks of sexual attraction.

Her eyes widened. No! Travis Eden was a rodeo cowboy, the lowest form of life on earth.

But she couldn't deny the signs. She felt the same way she'd felt eight years ago, when Bud Sager would look at her or touch her or kiss her. Except with Travis the feelings were stronger, deeper, hotter.

Dang. What was she going to do?

Avoid him, that's what. Out of sight, out of mind worked with Bud. It would work with Travis, too.

Finally they reached an open clerk.

Becca had just opened her mouth to ask for a room when Travis came up beside her.

"I want to make sure you get a room," he explained when she gave him a hard look.

Becca shrugged and turned to the clerk. "We need a room, please."

The woman looked tired and irritated. "What name is your reservation in, please?"

"We don't have a reservation. We were

planning on camping, you see, but our truck broke . . ." She trailed away as the woman shook her head.

"I'm sorry. We've been booked for a month. I don't have anything to give you until Wednesday."

"But we —"

"I'm sorry, ma'am. There's nothing I can do."

Becca felt her muscles droop with fatigue. "I guess we'll have to try one of the other hotels around. . . ."

The clerk shook her head again. "You won't find anything on the Strip, and downtown's even worse. There are several major conventions in town. The closest thing available is on the north side of town."

"The north side of town? But we don't have any way to get there. Or any way to get to the arena every day. Our truck broke down and —"

"I'm sorry, ma'am. You'll have to take a cab," she said without a hint of sympathy.

Becca saw dollar signs flash before her eyes. Taking a cab back and forth every day would severely cut into her bank account. "But I —"

Travis leaned across the counter. "I'm Travis Eden."

The clerk looked at him without a trace of recognition. "Do *you* have a reservation?"

"Yes, ma'am, I do."

"Then I can help you." She turned back to Becca. "I'm sorry, ma'am. If you'll just step aside so this gentleman can fill out his —"

"You've got to help us," Becca said fervently. "We don't have any other choice."

Travis grabbed one of the fists Becca banged on the marble counter. He couldn't leave the Larsons stranded. "Put them in my suite."

Becca turned to him with an open mouth. "What?"

"We can't take your room," Mrs. Larson said. "Where will you stay?"

"I'll stay there with you."

Becca gasped. "Now wait just a minute, buster —"

"There are four bedrooms," Travis said, cutting off her hot remark. "Hank, Alex and the kids take up the other two. We usually use the fourth room for the kids to play in, but there's plenty of room in the living area."

She shook her head firmly, making the curls framing her face bounce. "No, we couldn't. You've done too much already.

Besides, we couldn't possibly afford even a fourth of what a suite must cost."

"It's free. Part of my payment for making all those appearances." He pointed at the sign she'd turned her nose up at earlier. "One of the perks of being the Diamond Spurs Million-Dollar Cowboy."

"Surely your family could use the room."

Suddenly the plan that had occurred to Travis on the spur of the moment seemed perfect. What better way to keep the Larsons close so he could convince them he needed the Circle E more than they did? "I already told you, we don't really use it. Hank and Alex would be the first to offer it to you. In fact, they'll have my hide if you don't take it."

Joy Larson laid a hand on her daughter's arm. "It would save us a lot of money, dear. And you know we need every penny if we're going to —"

"I know, Momma," Becca said quickly, cutting off whatever her mother was going to say. "But what's it going to look like? Some people might get the wrong idea."

Travis lifted a brow and challenged, "About what?"

"About two single women sharing a suite with a notorious bachelor."

He grinned. "Notorious?"

"You're a rodeo cowboy, aren't you?"

"Just because all the cows are Angus, doesn't mean they're all black."

Obviously understanding his reproof on stereotyping, Becca opened her mouth to retort, but he cut her off. "You don't have to worry about your golden reputation. Hank and Alex will be there to protect you and your mother from the big bad wolf."

A wrinkle appeared between Becca's brows as she turned an alarmed, pleading gaze on her mother.

"You got a better plan?" he demanded.

"No. But I —"

"You what?"

Her chin rose. "I just wonder what you want in return."

"Becca!" her mother exclaimed.

Guilt made Travis's eyes narrow, and he suddenly remembered how good she'd been at reading him when they were kids. It was almost like there'd been a psychic connection of some kind. But that was years ago. They didn't know each other at all anymore. "Tell you what. You're dead set there's got to be payment of some kind. I've got a proposition for you."

Her eyes narrowed. "What kind of proposition?"

"I promised Hank and Alex I'd look after their kids during the day when I don't have sponsor obligations. Hank has quite a bit of business to take care of while he's here, and I just like to give the two of them some time alone. You help me with those kids, and we'll be square."

"You mean baby-sit J.J., Matt and Sarah?" she asked thoughtfully. "They're sweet kids. But —"

"We can do that, can't we, Becca?" Mrs. Larson said.

The panic returned to Becca's eyes. "Well, sure we can, but —"

"You're a good man, Travis. A true gentleman." Mrs. Larson extended her hand and smiled, though her face looked even more pinched than when he picked them up off the highway. "If you're sure we won't be putting you out by taking the room, we're much obliged."

Becca released a defeated groan, which Travis ignored.

"My pleasure, Mrs. Larson." He touched the brim of his hat and smiled at the older lady. "Well, I see the manager of the hotel. I'd better go check in with him. Can you ladies get up to the room okay?"

"I think we can manage," Becca said dryly.

"Good. I'll probably be a while."

"Here, then, we'll take your bag up." She grudgingly held out a hand.

His eyebrow shot up. This was the first nice gesture she'd made toward him.

"Don't look at me that way," she said hotly. "It'll just be in your way, and we're going up anyway."

Travis didn't hand it over. Instead, he whistled at a bellhop who pushed a large luggage cart their way. Travis handed him the room key and a ten. "Show these ladies to our suite. We're on the side next to the wet bar. Put my bag in the room with the king-size bed."

"Yes sir."

"But —"

Before Becca could object further, Travis turned and walked away.

While the bellhop placed the luggage in the proper bedrooms, the Larsons stood in the middle of Travis's suite, gaping.

"Have you ever?" Joy asked softly.

Becca hadn't ever seen anything like it in her entire life. This was not how people lived who considered a night at Motel Six a luxury.

The suite took up an entire end of the twenty-fifth floor. This central room was as big as three regular hotel rooms. The soft southwestern decor stretched from the table with thick, upholstered chairs all the way across the room to the sitting area boasting no less than three plush couches and four chairs. The bank of floor-to-ceiling windows stretching across the outer wall had two sliding glass doors which led onto a balcony that looked north up the Las Vegas Strip. A mini-kitchen stood to the left of the entrance and a wide-screen television stood in an alcove on the other side of a bathroom.

And they hadn't even looked in the bedrooms yet.

"Will there be anything else?" the bellhop asked as he reappeared.

Becca shook away the shock. "No, thank you." She dug into her purse for a tip and held it out as he passed.

"Mr. Eden took care of it, ma'am." He handed over the card that served as a room key. "Have a nice stay."

"Thank you," Becca murmured with a frown. Travis was good at taking care of things. He'd been doing it ever since she'd known him.

"I hate to touch anything," her mother exclaimed as the door closed behind the bellhop.

"Let's look at our room," Becca suggested.

They went through the door the bellhop had left open right next to the wet bar. Becca breathed a sigh of relief. This looked like any other nice hotel room with two double beds, a small couch and a dresser with a normal size television. There were two doors on the right side of the room, the folding door obviously a closet. She pushed open the other door and flipped on the light switch.

There was a mirror covering one wall above a long faux marble vanity with two sinks. A toilet and small shower stall were on the other wall.

"Dang. Where am I going to soak my aching muscles?" Becca said. "Looks like a place this fancy would have a tub, doesn't it?"

Her mother stood in the open door on the other side of the bathroom. "Look at this."

Becca joined her mother. "Dang."

Three steps led up to a tub big enough for two people. Mirrors covered the walls around it and silk plants added lushness.

Joy ran her hands along the chrome jets on the side. "Whirlpool. That should heal your aching muscles real good. This is the kind of place where movie stars stay. Can you imagine how much it costs?"

Becca frowned. "I don't want to even think about it."

Suddenly a ringing phone brought their heads around. The sound came through the door that evidently led to Travis's room.

"Should we answer it?" Joy asked.

"It's got to be for Travis. We shouldn't butt into his business."

"On the other hand, he might be grateful if we took a message." Joy's hands fluttered. "It's the least we can do for all of this."

Becca frowned at her mother. She hated being beholden to anyone, much less a rodeo cowboy, but her mother was right. If playing secretary might repay him in some small way, it was little enough for her to do.

With a sigh, she opened the door to Travis's bathroom, then the door to his room. Though the same size as theirs, it sported a king-size bed and a door leading onto a private balcony.

The phone rang again, and Becca walked to the bedside table and picked up the receiver. "Hello?"

Dead silence returned her greeting.

"Hello? Anyone there?"

"Is this Travis Eden's room?" asked a vaguely familiar feminine voice.

"Yes, it is. Travis isn't here right now. He caught up with the manager when we were checking in."

There was another pause. "Who is this?"

Becca bristled at the indignant tone. "Who is this?"

"I'm Alex Eden. Travis is my brother-in-law."

Becca relaxed. "Alex? I'm sorry. I didn't recognize your voice. I thought you were . . . well, you can guess who I thought you were. That'll teach me to jump to conclusions. This is Becca Larson, by the way."

"Becca? Oh. What are . . . Oh, dear. How do I ask this delicately?"

Becca chuckled. She'd liked Alex from the first moment they met. "What the heck am I doing in Travis's suite? I've been asking myself the same question for the last fifteen minutes."

"What?"

She sighed and explained why they'd be neighbors in the hotel as well as on the ranch.

"Sounds like Travis," Alex said with a smile in her voice. "I'm so glad there will be a couple more women in the suite — Sarah, no! Don't touch that, it's hot —

Sorry, she gets into everything."

"I remember. She's adorable. As a matter of fact, my mother and I will be baby-sitting your kids some this week, if you don't mind. Travis suggested it as a way to repay him for the room."

Alex chuckled. "Mind? I love my kids, but any break is welcome. I'll have to kiss Travis when we get there for thinking about it. And speaking of Travis, can you give him a message for me?"

"Sure."

"He's expecting us Saturday, but we won't make it until Monday. One of the geldings Hank is bringing came up lame this morning."

Becca frowned. There went the chaperones. "That's too bad. I hope he didn't have to be put down."

"Oh, no. The farrier was here yesterday and evidently nicked the quick of the gelding's hoof. Hank pulled out the nail and said he'd be okay, but he wanted to wait a couple of days before we haul him over six hundred miles. Anyway, Travis was going to meet us at the Whitehead ranch to help us unload, and we don't want to keep him waiting when we're not going to be there. Would you let him know we'll get in Monday afternoon?"

"No problem," Becca assured her.

An audible sigh came over the phone. "Thanks. I really appreciate it. I've been trying to reach him all afternoon. He should've gotten there around noon, by Hank's reckoning."

"He stopped to help us," Becca reminded her.

"Yes, I know that now. Anyway, we'll take you and your mother to lunch one day next week."

"You don't have to do that. It's just —"

"But I want to," Alex insisted. "I'll see you when we get in."

"Bye." Becca replaced the phone thoughtfully, then walked back into their room.

"Who was that, dear?" Her mother was unpacking their bags.

"Alex Eden." Becca lifted her mother's bag — which was the heaviest — onto the bed. "She said they won't be in until Monday. A problem with one of the horses they're bringing to sell."

"So we'll have this big ol' place to ourselves a couple of days." Her mother turned to an open drawer of the dresser and dropped the stack of underwear into it — only she missed. "Oh, dear."

"Momma," Becca breathed. She took

her mother by the shoulders and gently turned her around. She'd been too distracted to look closely at her mother since the truck broke down, but now she saw the signs she'd come to dread — the pale face, the pinched lips and the faraway look in her eyes — as if Joy Larson would rather be anywhere but inside her body. That look scared Becca more than anything.

"You have another headache, don't you?"

Tears sprang to her mother's blue eyes, which were identical to her own. "I'm sorry, Becca. I know how much all this means to you. I wanted to be well for you this week."

Tears stinging her own eyes, Becca hugged her mother. "Oh, Momma, you can't help it."

"But I wanted to be strong so I could watch you ride."

Grief stabbed Becca so deep she felt pinned to the floor. "It's all right, Momma. There are ten go-rounds in the Finals. Your headaches only last a few days at a time." Although they'd been lasting longer and longer the past few months. "Besides, you're wrong. The only thing being here means is making enough money to pay off our loan, so we can go home to stay."

Home to die. Neither of them had ever actually said the words, but they both knew that's what it meant for Joy Larson. Two years ago, doctors had given her a year to live because of a tumor growing inside her brain. The doctors refused to operate because the chances were too great Joy would die on the operating table.

With shaking hands, Joy framed her daughter's face. "You've worked so hard. I know you've done it all for me, to let me spend my last few days —"

"Hush, Momma," Becca begged.

Joy briefly closed her eyes. "This needs to be said, dear. I want you to know I'm grateful. If it turns out we lose the Circle E again —"

"We won't," Becca insisted. "I'm going to win the championship."

Joy searched her daughter's face. "I love you, Rebecca Edith Larson. A woman couldn't ask for a better daughter."

Pain so deep she couldn't name it stole Becca's breath. Her mother was all she had left. What was she going to do when Joy Larson was no longer in this world?

Then she felt her mother trembling, and strength surged back into her own muscles. Strength to do what needed to be done, with no help from anyone. Like always.

Easing her mother back onto the bed closest to the window, she urged her down. She closed the curtains and lowered the lights, then helped her mother into her nightgown. Before tucking Joy in, Becca watched her swallow the strong painkillers that would put her to sleep, the only thing that gave any relief.

Becca held her mother's thin hand as Joy drifted away, making certain the tears streaming down her face were silent.

Chapter Three

Wednesday, Welcome Reception

Left to himself for the first time since he'd arrived in Las Vegas, Travis glanced around the crowded Riviera Hotel ballroom. People were packed into the room like cattle in a holding pen. The only times he'd seen this many people in one place, they were safely held back by an arena fence. Men outnumbered women at least three to one.

Speaking of women, where were the Larsons? The contestants had already made their trips across the stage, shaking the hands of rodeo dignitaries while receiving their back numbers and NFR bomber-style jackets. He'd watched Becca cross the stage after him, then a fan came up wanting an autograph and he'd lost sight of her.

Had she found her mother in this mob? They might already be heading back to the hotel. He needed to cut them off at the pass. It was time to start the wining and dining.

To his surprise, he actually looked forward to their seduction more than he'd —

Seduction? Why the hell had he used that word?

Becca's face suddenly sprang to mind, and Travis groaned. He couldn't think of Becca in those terms. He —

"Travis Eden! I've been looking all over for you!"

Trying not to roll his eyes, Travis turned toward the too-friendly voice, but was pleasantly surprised to see not another reporter, but an old Wyoming acquaintance, Ote Duggan. Closer to Hank's age than Travis's, Ote was Sam Duggan's nephew. Ote had moved out of Dubois after high school and had done well as a banker in Riverton. Unlike his uncle, Ote was a reasonable man. He didn't blame Travis for his cousin's death.

Travis's grin widened and he shook Ote's hand firmly. "Bless my spurs. Ote Duggan. What are you doing down here?"

"My boy was hot to come. He's just started Little Britches competition, you know."

"No, I didn't. Where is he?"

Ote stuck his thumbs in his belt loops.

"He's running around trying to get everybody's autograph. He'll make it around to you. Don't worry."

"Are you here for all ten go-rounds?"

Ote shook his head. "Just till Monday. Marty's momma won't let him miss that much school."

"Well, it's good to see you."

"Listen, I was hoping I'd run into you while we were here," Ote said, suddenly serious. "I've been trying to reach you for two weeks, but Hank said you were on the road."

Travis nodded, his smile frozen into place. Ote wanted something.

Why should he be surprised? Since Travis had made it big, everyone wanted something — donations for charity, appearances at rodeos or store openings. He did what he could, but he'd been chipped away at for so long, he was beginning to feel as if there wasn't anything left.

"I've got a proposition you might be interested in," Ote said.

Here it comes.

"You remember that old ranch my uncle bought way back around fifteen years or so ago? It was a bankruptcy. Redheaded fellow named Hoyt Larson."

Travis straightened. "The Circle E."

"Yeah, that's it. I was going through my uncle's things and found a note you wrote years ago, saying as how you wanted to buy that land and all. I was just wondering if you were still interested."

Suddenly Ote had his full attention. "Hell, yes, I'm still interested. But what about the Larsons? Your uncle sold the Circle E back to them last summer."

"Rebecca's the only one named on the papers, but she didn't get a regular loan, see. My uncle financed the deal himself. Now I'm a banker, you know, and I've been looking over the situation now that my uncle has gone to his reward, being his beneficiary and all." Ote shook his head. "Miss Larson's got no collateral whatsoever 'cept a nice little mare and a beat-up old truck. Just doesn't make good business sense, so I've called in the loan."

Shock nearly made Travis lose his smile. Here was his chance to own the land he'd hankered after since he was a boy. How many years had it been since he'd had even the remotest hope of purchasing the Circle E?

Elation made his blood pump as fast as the legs of stampeding horses. He knew exactly where he wanted to build his log house — far enough down the south side of Yellow Jack Mountain to be protected from the worst weather, yet high enough for a view. He even had the blueprints for the house. He'd purchased them six years ago, certain he'd wear Sam Duggan down eventually. That hadn't happened, but now —

His excitement came to a screeching halt as Ote's last words sank in. *Called in the loan.* The Larsons were losing the Circle E. Again.

Travis's smile vanished as he remembered the day fifteen years ago when Mrs. Larson received the news her land was going to be auctioned. He was seventeen and had come over to the Circle E to help with chores, like he did just about every day back then. He found Mrs. Larson slumped against the kitchen wall, tears streaming down her face, the phone receiver still clutched in her hand.

Alarmed to learn someone could lose their family home so easily, Travis had talked to everyone in town, trying to get them to help. But the residents of the Wind River Valley all had their own troubles, and the bankers wouldn't listen to a seventeen-year-old boy. Travis raised a few hundred dollars, but it wasn't nearly enough.

He'd stood by Becca and Mrs. Larson on the day their property was auctioned — almost a man, but with no resources to save the ranch for the small family who had become as dear to him as his own. The Circle E had been Joy and Becca Larson's birthplace, their birthright. Travis's own grandfather had sold it to Mrs. Larson's father forty-six years before, and it was all taken away with the hammer of a gavel.

"What do you say?" Ote pressed. "Wanna shake hands on it?"

Travis felt a sudden aversion to the man who'd once been a friend. How could Ote rip people's lives apart like this? How could he take away the Larsons' land?

Ote, hell. How could Travis take it away?

He remembered his plan to sweet-talk Becca and her mother into selling him the Circle E. But that was different. He'd have given them a fair deal. This . . .

He didn't like this one damn bit.

Ote's eyes began to narrow. "Thought you said you were interested. If you aren't, I got several other people that'll take it off my hands."

"Who?" Travis challenged. "Your uncle never got an offer all these years. That land's too remote. He only used it as a hunting club."

Ote's lips pursed. "The interest is offshore."

"Offshore? You mean foreign? Hell, Ote, you gonna sell American land to some guy who can't even speak English?"

"If he's got American dollars, I am. I need the money, Travis. Banking ain't what it used to be. Not in our neck of the woods."

"How much do the Larsons owe?"

Ote named the sum.

Travis's frown deepened. "Becca would have to win the barrel racing championship to get that much money."

"Yeah, well, anything's possible. I gave her till December thirty-first to pay off the loan. But this is her first run at a title, and how many rookies take home a gold buckle? Only two that I heard tell of." Ote shook his head. "The Circle E's as good as yours if you want it."

Travis's eyes drifted out over the crowded room. Want the Circle E? Hell, of course he wanted it. But not like this.

On the other hand, if he didn't take Ote up on his offer, somebody else would. It was too close to what happened ten years ago when the Edens nearly lost their own family ranch, the Garden, to foreign investment. He'd fought to save the Garden then, and he'd do whatever he could now to save the land that had once been part of the Garden.

He had to, for the sake of his own sanity.

Though the notion wouldn't make sense to any sane man, Travis had begun to believe during the past few years that if he made the Garden whole again by buying the Circle E, he'd make himself whole again.

He'd wanted to retire for the last four or five years. He was tired of driving through the night pushing to get to the next rodeo, tired of performing for the crowds, tired of being pulled at from all directions. He'd played rodeo star so long, sometimes he wondered if the real Travis Eden would ever be heard from again. Sometimes he wondered if he even knew who the real Travis Eden was.

Trouble was, the only place for him to retire to was the Garden. He loved Hank and his family, but being around them reminded Travis that he didn't have anyone who thought he'd hung the moon in the nighttime sky, like Alex thought of Hank. Travis needed a place of his own, a place where he could be alone, a place where he could find himself again. Maybe then he could find someone to share his life with, someone who wanted Travis Eden the man, not the Million-Dollar Cowboy.

The Circle E was the place he wanted. Not only had it once been part of the Garden, it was close enough for Travis to help Hank with the family business of training rodeo horses, but far enough away for him to find solitude when he needed it.

At that moment the sea of humanity shifted, and he spied Becca talking to Chance just a few yards away. She didn't look happy about the cowboy's hand on her arm.

How happy would she be when she found out Travis was responsible for her losing her ranch for the second time?

But, hell. If Ote was going to foreclose anyway, what else could he do but buy the land?

He was damned if he did, and damned if he didn't.

That being the case, Travis slowly turned back to Ote and offered his hand. "I don't like the situation, but I'm not going to sit by and watch the Circle E go to some foreigner. I've wanted it too long."

With a broad smile, Ote shook his hand firmly. "I knew I could count on you."

Travis wondered if the Larsons thought

the same thing. "Yeah, well, I gotta go."

He spun on his heel, wanting just to get the hell of out there and think. But as he turned he caught another glimpse of Becca, surrounded by three cowboys who were in on Chance's stupid bet. They were closing in on her like a pack of wolves on wounded prey.

Anger swept through him at the thought of their grimy claws on her lovely, pale skin.

Travis froze in mid-stride, startled by the powerful feeling of protectiveness. He quickly rationalized it by remembering what he'd just discovered.

Becca Larson had been through enough. He'd be damned before he let anyone else hurt her.

Shoving away the thought that he'd made a bargain to do just that, Travis shouldered his way through the crowd.

"Hey, you're going the wrong way," Chance said as he captured Becca's arm.

She wrinkled her nose and fanned away beer fumes. "Chance Morgan, you've been drinking."

"Just a couple of beers." His arm slid around her waist. "But I could use another one. Come on. I'm buying."

Becca placed her hands square on his chest and shoved. "I'm trying to find Travis."

"What for?" Chance grumbled. "He ain't no fun. Me, on the other hand —"

"Which other hand? You've got forty!" Becca shrugged her shoulders out from under his arm. When he made no further move to manhandle her, she relaxed. "Have you seen Travis or not?"

"He's over there talking to some guy," Kevin said. Just a few inches taller than Becca, Kevin had little pig eyes in a face that looked as if someone had flattened it with a frying pan.

Becca peered in the direction Kevin pointed and caught a glimpse of Travis. He was shaking hands with a barrel-shaped man with a gray hat. Was it Ote Duggan? The man was turned away from her so she couldn't seen him very well, and she'd only seen the Riverton banker once. What would he be doing here?

She took a step in their direction. Before Joy had succumbed to the drugs, she made Becca promise to deliver Alex's message to Travis personally. She came up short when Wade's hand caught her by the brand-new jacket she held over her arm.

"Where ya going?" His breath carried

the distinctly sweet smell of whisky.

Becca swatted his hand away. "I need to see Travis."

Kevin sneered as he stepped into her path. "He ain't ready to go up to bed yet."

Becca gasped, then narrowed her eyes. She knew that's what people would think when they heard she was sharing a suite with Travis. Evidently the word had already spread. "You let me by, Kevin Chapman, or so help me I'll tell your father. What do you think *Reverend* Chapman would say about you talking like that to me?"

"Hell, Kevin don't care," Chance blustered.

Becca didn't take her eyes off the Kansas preacher's son. "Oh, no?"

Kevin's little pig eyes narrowed to slits. "We was only foolin'. You ain't got no cause spreading lies to my —"

"Howdy, boys."

The deep cool voice cut through the noise of the room. They all turned to see Travis standing behind Kevin. "You boys keeping my date company?"

Travis held out a hand to Becca, and her eyes widened. His *date?*

The sky blue eyes surveyed the three cowboys, then locked into hers. His message was clear. He was saving her. Again.

Becca hesitated. She *had* begun to feel trapped by the three inebriated cowboys, and concerned about how aggressive they were becoming, even in such a crowded room.

Reluctantly she reached for Travis's hand. His warm fingers closed around hers, and he gently pulled her to his side. Becca felt him relax, and her own muscles melted in response.

"I've been waiting for you, darlin'. What's been keeping you?"

Darling? Becca looked up to find his smiling face mere inches from hers. Heat flowed through her entire body. "I . . . um . . . couldn't find you."

"I said to meet me at the east wall after the ceremony. Don't you know your directions?"

Becca's gaze shifted around to Chance, Kevin and Wade. All three frowned at Travis's performance, so she improvised. "I must've gotten turned around when I walked off the stage."

He shrugged. "We found each other, that's what matters. You ready?"

"I guess so," she said softly.

Travis lifted his head and stared down each of the three drunk cowboys. Disgust made a muscle in his jaw twitch. All three were involved in the wager on who could melt Becca's icicles first. Were they stepping up the pressure?

Combined with the deal he'd just made, the possibility made Travis want to punch something . . . hard.

Chance was the last cowboy he faced down.

"You sure work fast," the header said belligerently. "I heard she was staying in your room."

Travis squeezed Becca's hand when she gasped. He didn't like his team roping partner very much right now, but they had to stay on friendly terms through the next week if they had any hope of winning the championship. "She and her mother are sharing one of the spare rooms in my suite. Hank, Alex and the kids are taking the other ones. You got a problem with that?"

Chance's muddy brown eyes slid away, but he didn't sound happy when he said, "Reckon not."

"Good. See you boys later." Shifting for a firmer grasp on Becca's hand, he drew her toward one of the doors.

"What the heck was that all about?" Becca demanded when they were halfway out of the room.

He glanced at her as he wove between tight-packed groups of people. He'd already decided it was best not to tell her about the wager, but he didn't want to lie. "You looked like you needed rescuing."

Becca tried unsuccessfully to pull her hand from his. "Okay, you rescued me. You can let go now and get back to smiling at the cameras."

He stopped but didn't release her hand. "I'm through with cameras for the night. I thought we'd grab something to eat before we head back to the hotel. Where's your mother?"

Her gaze focused someplace over his shoulder. "She's not here."

"Your first National Finals and she didn't come watch you get your number? That doesn't sound like the Joy Larson I know. She used to be proud of every little thing you did. Hell, you couldn't see the refrigerator for all the pictures of horses you drew."

"Momma has a headache." The understatement came easily to Becca. Since neither one of them wanted to be objects of pity, she and her mother had agreed not to tell anyone about Joy's condition. "And you haven't seen us for fifteen years. You don't know either one of us."

“Have you changed so much, monkey-face?” he asked quietly.

So they were back to monkey-face. Yet somehow his low, rumbling voice made the words an endearment even more intimate than “darling.” Becca fought the urge to move closer. Travis’s deep voice was an echo of her father’s. The pleasure the tones sent through her reminded her of a time when she still loved her father, before she knew how his obsession with rodeo would ruin their lives.

Travis had the same obsession. How else could he have climbed to the top of rodeo’s rocky mountain — the summit her father had aspired to, but never reached?

She took a step away. “Yes, we’ve changed. And so have you.”

“What is it the French say? Something about hooray for the difference.” His smiled softened. “I’m looking forward to getting acquainted all over again.”

Becca frowned. If he thought they were going to renew their friendship of long ago, he had a few more thinks coming. When they were kids, she’d followed him around like an adoring puppy. That wasn’t going to happen again. He was a rodeo cowboy. She had as much use for a rodeo cowboy as she did a cracked saddle tree. “You don't have to do this, Travis. I know you're busy with sponsors and family and everything. We thank you for the room, but we'll be okay on our own."

His smile slipped a notch. "But I want —"

"Travis Eden! Finally! Over here, guys!"

They turned to find a microphone with the letters ESPN shoved in Travis's face. A bright light beamed from the side of a camera behind a petite brunette woman dressed in a red suit and a lot of make-up.

Without preliminary, the reporter started in. "Travis, not only are you a shoo-in for All-Around Cowboy this year, but you're also up for two more gold buckles in team roping and bull riding. You could win three gold buckles. Think it's possible?"

Travis didn't miss a beat. "Well, Linda, anything's possible. A lot depends on the stock I draw." His smile widened. "And fourteen other cowboys cooperating by having ten bad days."

The reporter's smile widened, too, though Becca couldn't tell whether it was a response to Travis's sexy grin or gratitude for a good sound bite. Whichever it was, it made her skin tighten.

"Not only are you making history by being up for three buckles, but you've won the bull riding championship seven times in the past twelve years, and you're up for number eight, tying Don Gay's world record. Can you do it?"

As Travis continued answering questions in the amusing, self-deprecating way he was famous for, his voice held far more of a cowboy twang than it did when he was talking to her. Becca backed up a step and tried again to retake possession of her hand. Travis wouldn't let go. She sent her best frown his way, but he wasn't paying her any mind.

Her attention caught by his posturing for the camera, she was suddenly struck by the width of his smile. A little too wide. She didn't know how, but she knew it was fake. A mask.

The only question was, what was it hiding?

Suddenly Becca wanted to know. She wanted to peel away the layers Travis had built up during the past fifteen years. Was there anything left of the boy she'd worshipped? Or was he now — as she suspected — just another rodeo cowboy?

One thing about him hadn't changed — his eagerness to help. Had any of his other qualities survived all these years on the rodeo circuit?

As Travis gave the reporter the answers she wanted, Becca thought back fifteen, twenty years. When she was a little girl, Travis had been so much a part of her life that she'd never questioned his presence. He came to the Circle E almost daily. She didn't know then how much he was giving to her and her mother, how valuable the time he spent doing the chores only a man could handle — a man they couldn't afford to hire.

But she knew now, just as she knew the value of help he'd given them today. The hotel room alone was worth hundreds of dollars.

She could never come close to repaying him for what he'd done, and that troubled her more than anything else.

Becca hated being a charity case. The aversion came from their poverty during the years right after she and her mother lost the ranch. She'd been eleven when the Circle E was auctioned — old enough to know the looks sent their way were pity, to see the desperation in her mother's eyes, to feel the pain of saying goodbye to the barrel racing horse her father had bought for her. She'd been plunged into the icy depths of reality that awful day, and she'd been struggling to swim back to the surface ever since. It seemed like every time she made it and took a gasp of air, another rock was thrown around her neck, dragging her under again.

"— known Travis all your life?"

The microphone was shoved in her face, startling Becca back to the present. Not only was she the focal point for the camera, but Travis, the reporter and everyone around stared at her. "I'm sorry. Could you repeat the question?"

The reporter rolled her eyes. "Travis said he helped you up onto your first barrel racing horse. That he's known you all your life. Can you tell me why you just showed up at PRCA rodeos at the end of last year?"

When Becca looked at Travis, his smile softened. He was thrusting her into the limelight. Well, she needed all the exposure she could get to make her plans for a barrel racing school successful, so she could support herself and her mother on the ranch.

She turned back to the reporter. What could she say? Certainly not that she'd hated rodeo ever since she realized that it — or rather her father's love for it — had ruined their lives. She couldn't say that she'd only started barrel racing again so she could earn extra money, and only joined the Professional Rodeo Cowboys Association a year ago so she could enter the rodeos with the biggest payoffs and buy back the Circle E. Still, part of the truth would be best.

"I lost my horse and had to wait until the perfect one came along. Cocoa is the best barrel racer I've ever seen."

"Did you train her yourself?" the reporter asked.

Becca nodded. "From the day she was born."

The reporter asked another question of Travis then, and Becca breathed a sigh of relief. Travis must've felt it, because he squeezed her hand gently as he replied to the reporter.

The simple gesture sent emotions tumbling through Becca. She'd forgotten there'd once been a time when someone knew her well enough to know when she was nervous, who cared enough to give encouragement. Oh, her mother cared, but during the past few years all their focus had necessarily been on Joy and her illness. Becca had to be the strong one, and she'd had to do it alone.

She'd forgotten how good it felt to have someone who wanted to help.

Too bad that someone was a rodeo cowboy.

Travis threw back the covers and stalked, naked, to the bank of windows. At two forty-seven in the morning, the Las Vegas Strip was still bright with lights, teeming with people and cars.

He needed to sleep. He had several special appearances that day. But every time he closed his eyes guilt ate at him like a winter-starved herd ate a field of spring grass.

What the hell was he going to do about the Larsons? No matter what he told Ote Duggan, he couldn't buy their ranch out from under them. He was a lot of things, but not a low-down, dirty backstabber.

Besides, Hank and Alex would never speak to him again.

What could he do? The easiest thing would be to lend the Larsons the money to pay off the loan, then talk them into selling the ranch to him.

Travis shook his head. Becca would never take enough money from him to pay off her loan, even if he charged her interest. Her hackles went up every time he offered to buy her a soft drink.

Which made Travis frown as he thought about it. He was just trying to be a nice guy, but she acted like he wanted something in return.

Which he did — the Circle E.

Damn. She was right to be suspicious of him.

So how was he going to help her pay off the damn loan?

Though he stared blindly at the lights for a long time, the answer eluded him. She had to win the money, because she wouldn't take it any other way. If she didn't win, she'd lose the ranch. But the odds against a rookie winning the championship were very high.

Unless . . .

Maybe he could help her win.

How? He didn't know anything about barrel racing except the basics, and he was damn sure someone who'd made it to the National Finals had the fundamentals down.

On the other hand, he knew people who were intimately familiar with all the nuances of the sport. Even if Becca wouldn't let them help her — which he had a sneaking suspicion she wouldn't — he could ask them to watch her and give him some pointers. Hell, he'd pay someone if he had to, but he didn't think he'd have to. He'd done enough favors for people over the years. Time to start calling in his markers.

The main thing he had to do was keep Becca focused. That's what it took to win a championship.

Travis straightened and headed back to bed, feeling much better about himself.

He could do this. He could own the Circle E without becoming a sidewinder in the process. All he had to do was help Becca win the championship. A hard task, but not impossible.

He would also step up his wining and dining campaign, so he could plant seeds about him needing the ranch more than she did. They were going to be spending a lot of time together during the next ten days. Might as well rope two steers with one loop.

As he settled beneath the covers, he remembered taking her out for supper after the welcoming ceremony. Once he'd gotten past her objections, they'd had fun.

Like old times. Only better. Much, much better.

He frowned as he laced his fingers behind his head.

He was going to have to be careful. The last thing he needed right now was an emotional attachment. He needed time for himself — all by himself — before he'd be good for anybody.

Chapter Four

Thursday

The elevator door slid open, and Travis stopped cold.

"Travis, honey! About time you came down."

His smile tightened as he cringed inside. "CherylAnn. What are you doing here?"

He stepped briskly into the room crowded with people held up by one-armed bandits, but CherylAnn managed to link her arm through his.

"I want to talk to you, Travis, honey. Alone. Slow down a little, okay?"

"I've got a special appearance in five minutes."

"I know. That's why I waited by the elevator." She pulled him to a stop by an empty blackjack table and batted her eyelashes up at him. "Can we meet somewhere later? I've got a room to myself at the Las Vegas Club."

"No, CherylAnn. I'm not interested in anything you have to say." He wrenched his arms from her claws and headed for the kids' area.

She followed as he pushed through the crowd. "Travis, honey, you don't mean that," she called over the loud dinging of a slot machine paying off.

"Like hell I don't. It's over, CherylAnn. Find yourself another sucker. There's got to be one or two cowboys in the PRCA you haven't slept with yet."

Resorting to melodrama — her favorite tactic — CherylAnn threw her arms in the air. "But I love you, Travis. I really, really do."

He halted abruptly, cussing under his breath. She obviously took that as an encouraging sign, because she grabbed his hand. He yanked it away. "You don't love anybody or anything but yourself. I may have learned that lesson the hard way, but I learned it real good. No hard feelings. Good luck with the Finals and with your life. Just leave me the hell alone."

She stiffened, hands clenched at her sides, as if stricken with sudden rigor mortis. "It's Becca Larson, isn't it? She stole you away from me."

"Nobody stole me away, and you know

it. Hell, CherylAnn, I caught you in bed with two cowboys."

"You told me you weren't going to ride in Oklahoma City that week."

He rolled his eyes. "And that made it okay? We were engaged."

Tears caught in her whisky-brown eyes. "I know. I'm sorry, Travis. I promise I'll never do anything like that again."

"I don't care what you do." He wheeled around and resumed his path toward the back of the casino.

"I won't give up," she called after him. "I'm gonna win you back if it's the last thing I do!"

Travis pulled his hat lower and walked faster.

Friday, Go-Round #1

Becca eased the bedroom door closed. Her mother had finally fallen asleep after spending a day racked with pain. The usual dose of pills hadn't been enough today. Becca had finally talked her into taking twice the regular amount.

After two days of taking care of her mother, Becca was as exhausted as Joy. Only Becca couldn't go to sleep. Somehow, she had to find the energy to win the first go-round.

"You ready to go?"

With a gasp, Becca spun to find Travis at the door to his room, pulling his shirt from his jeans. She placed a hand over her heart. "Travis. I didn't hear you come in. Is it time to go already?"

He grabbed the front tails and yanked the snaps apart.

Startled by the sudden sight of a deeply muscled chest covered with a light mat of dark hair, her eyes widened.

"Grand entry starts at 6:45, and we need time to warm up our horses."

She dragged her eyes up from the line of hair that veed down a washboard stomach and disappeared into formfitting jeans. "All the go-rounds are at night, aren't they?"

"Except for the tenth, which has to end in time for the awards banquet." He smiled. "Nervous?"

He was making her more nervous by undressing before her eyes. "A little, I guess."

"Don't be. The crowd's not that much bigger than some of the larger rodeos." He glanced down as he opened his cuffs. "Come to think of it, why didn't I ever see you at Cheyenne or Fort Worth or any of the other big ones?"

She didn't want to get into why she didn't say anything to him all those times, not when she was distracted by the play of hard muscles under his tanned skin, not when she had to fight the desire to feel that movement for herself. "I . . . um . . . I guess we rode on different days. And you rough-stock riders don't stick around on the big weekends."

He acknowledged her statement with a shrug, which also served to free one arm of his shirt.

Finally she couldn't take any more of his striptease. "Why are you undressing in front of me?"

He glanced at her in surprise. "I've got to change into my lucky, first-night shirt. Does it bother you?"

"Yes!"

A sexy grin stole across his face. "Is your mom ready to go?"

Reminded of her mother, Becca glanced at the closed bedroom door. Dang. She couldn't believe he'd distracted her so easily. "Momma isn't going tonight."

Travis went still with his shirt halfway off. "She's not going to watch your first ride at the National Finals?"

Becca shook her head. "Her head still hurts pretty bad."

"She's been sick for two days. Is there anything I can do?"

She met his eyes. The concern in the deep blue depths was real.

A tiny shiver skimmed along her spine. How long had it been since someone offered to help? She couldn't remember the last time. But she could remember all the times this man had helped her and her mother in years past — and in the past two days.

She knew without a doubt his offer was genuine. She also knew she couldn't accept. Beyond the fact that she refused to take any more charity than absolutely necessary — and that only for her mother's sake — Travis had enough to worry about. This was their burden, and theirs alone. Besides, there wasn't anything he could do.

Becca shook her head again. "She's sleeping now."

"Is this normal?" Travis pressed. "Has she seen a doctor?"

"Yes, of course." She stuffed her hands in the pockets of her jeans. "There's not much you can do for migraines, except sleep until they pass."

He nodded, his comprehension obvious. Migraine headaches were something most people understood, so that's the explanation Becca used.

He finished dragging off his shirt and started back into his room. "Let me change and I'll be good to go."

Distracted again by the sight of his bare body, Becca swallowed hard. "Maybe I should catch a bus . . . or a cab . . . or something."

He turned with a raised brow. "No, you shouldn't. You're riding to the arena and back with me. Plus anywhere else we have to go. I know I haven't been around much the past two days. I always schedule the bulk of my appearances before the first go-round, so I can relax the rest of the week. So from now on, we'll have more time together." He paused, then added almost as an afterthought, "Monkey-face."

More time together? That's the last thing she wanted. "I'll take a cab if I want to."

He cocked his head slightly. "Why would you do that when I'm going to the same place at the same time, I have plenty of room and it's free?"

It was the "free" part that hit home. What was she doing? She'd never been one who cut off her nose to spite her face. Just since Travis Eden reappeared in her life. Once upon a time he'd brought out the best in her. Now he brought out the worst. Or maybe she was afraid to find he could still bring out her best — and that she'd like it.

Dismissing the notion, she lifted a brow. "Well, if you're going to make sense . . ."

His smile widened. "I'll be right out."

"Have a good time last night?"

Travis tore his gaze away from Becca, who slowly circled Cocoa inside the large tent set up just outside the Thomas and Mack Arena for contestants to warm up their horses. Kevin Chapman stood beside him, just inside the opening that served as a door to the makeshift arena. Kevin had practically sneered the question. Probably a result of his not having placed in the bareback riding, which had already taken place.

Travis shifted his eyes back to Becca. He and Chance had already won first place in team roping, now he was waiting for his turn to climb on top of a bull in the last event. "What's it to you, Kev?"

Kevin released a stream of tobacco juice into the dirt. "Hell, ain't nothing to me, Trav. But you ain't in on the bet, you know."

"No, and you shouldn't be, either."

Travis used to like Kevin, back when the Kansas cowboy had first made the jump to professional. Hell, Kevin probably wouldn't be a finalist without the advice Travis had given him those first few years.

Travis knew he'd changed, but he hadn't known how much until the past couple of days. Had he really been the same as Chance, Kevin and the others who'd come up with this bet? He hated the thought. "Seems to me you boys have way too much time on your hands. This bet is downright mean-spirited, and that's a fact."

"Hell, Trav, it's all in fun."

"Maybe from your point of view, but have you thought about it from hers?" He nodded toward Becca.

Kevin's eyes slid away. "It weren't my idea. Hell, it's just a joke."

"You put a hundred dollars of hard-earned money down on a joke?"

He shrugged. "I was drunk. Hell, we was all drunk. Chance is the one who came up with the notion. Why aren't you on his case?"

"Don't think I haven't been. I just wanted to hear your side."

"What's it to you anyway, Eden?" Kevin asked belligerently.

Travis hesitated. "Becca's a nice girl."

The Kansas bull rider snickered. "Rick Ivey said we'd be doing her a favor."

Travis shook his head. "What about your dad, Kevin? Think he'd be proud to know you're trying to seduce innocent young women?"

Kevin's eyes narrowed, and he shifted his wad of tobacco from one cheek to the other. "You ain't gonna tell him, are you, Trav? Hell, that'd be the pot calling the kettle black, now wouldn't it?"

Travis lowered the brim of his hat, and his eyes sought Becca. She leaned into her mare as they circled imaginary barrels, her cheeks painted like roses by the brisk December air.

How could he argue? He'd had his share of women over the eleven years of his professional rodeo career. More than his share, probably. Hell, the women hanging around rodeos weren't called buckle chasers for nothing. And Travis hadn't made a practice of running. He'd never had to do more than look behind the chutes at the end of any rodeo and crook his finger at the prettiest girl. They seemed eager enough, and God knew he'd been itching for a woman in his arms.

But the past couple of years he'd found himself crooking his finger less and less. A different girl every night just wasn't satisfying anymore — and one night was about all he could stand any of them.

"You ain't sweet on Becca, are you?" Kevin interrupted his thoughts. "Chance said you was pretending to be a gentleman, that you didn't care no more for Becca Larson than you did for CherylAnn Barnes."

"What else did my *buddy* say?" Travis used the well-known term for traveling partners loosely.

"That you'd get tired of hanging around Becca in a couple of days, just like every other woman you ever dated."

Travis started to tell Kevin that the only interest he had in Becca Larson was five hundred acres in the Wind Mountains of Wyoming, but he didn't. That would just encourage every cowboy in on the bet to hound her, when Becca needed to concentrate on winning.

What would it take to discourage these cowboys?

Then Kevin's earlier question caught in his mind. If he put his brand on Becca, no cowboy in the PRCA would dare touch her. But how could he do that? Having Becca as his woman would require touching her, kissing her. And though he wasn't averse at all to the idea, where would it lead? If he started holding her, he might never want to stop.

On the other hand, how many women had he held over the years? Becca probably wouldn't appeal to him any longer than the others. Hell, he was probably thinking about her so much only because he'd told himself he couldn't have her.

Maybe it would work if they just pretended to be a couple. That way he'd only touch her in public, and things couldn't get out of hand.

The more he thought about the idea, the more he liked it. Not only would these cowboys leave Becca alone, but CherylAnn would have to back off on him, too.

"What if I told you I was sweet on Becca?" Travis asked. "Would you still be trying to win the money?"

Kevin studied his face, all the while chewing his tobacco like a cow chewing its cud. "Don't sound like you're serious, Trav. But if I saw that you was, sure, I'd back off. I reckon I owe you too much to try to horn in on your heifer."

"Nice to know you still got some conscience left," Travis said wryly.

"But unless I see her hanging on your arm, Becca's fair game."

Travis cussed under his breath even as he nodded. This plan would require Becca's cooperation, and he had no idea how to convince her. He didn't want to tell her about the wager, and she'd made it plain she had no use for him or any other rodeo cowboy. Hell, she hadn't so much as glanced his way since she rode into the warm-up tent.

So how was he going to talk her into acting like she was in love with him?

Becca stepped down off the stage onto the dance floor of the darkened, crowded Western Dance Hall at the Gold Coast Hotel, clutching the box that held her first go-round buckle. Though it was almost midnight, she was no longer tired. The adrenaline of winning sang through her veins. She wished her mother could've been there to watch her walk up onto the stage and take the gentle ribbing the announcers dished out with the buckles.

Travis's blue eyes followed her as she wove through the hundreds of people packed into the room. Contestants. Fans. Media. They were here to see the winners. And she was one.

Though she hadn't thought it would, the buckle in her hand meant more to her than the first of ten steps to winning the championship she needed to pay off the loan on the ranch. Winning the first round of the National Finals plain felt good, even if she'd won by just six hundredths of a point. Winning meant she was better than fourteen other contestants, who were better than all the others in the world. Tonight, at least, she was on top.

Travis's ever-present smile widened as she came up beside him. "You looked great up there."

"Thanks." She smiled up at him, feeling generous. He'd already been on stage with Chance, receiving his buckle for team roping. "So did you."

He grinned as they announced his name for bull riding. "One more time."

Becca waited patiently as he took another turn on stage, giving the announcers as good a ribbing as they gave him about winning two events in the same night. For the first time she could watch him without being obvious and she took full advantage, staring until her eyes hurt from the bright stage lights.

Travis was undeniably handsome, with strong features and a square jaw. Though he had the well-proportioned body most working cowboys had, on Travis everything seemed so much bigger — from his broad shoulders to his tight hips to his strong, slightly bowed legs. Who would've thought the skinny boy she once knew would grow up into a larger-than-life hero?

Who would've thought she'd be so attracted to him?

The errant thought startled her. Attracted? To a rodeo cowboy? Not in this lifetime.

As he stepped down from the stage, she kept her eyes from following his progress by fastening them on the announcers as they wound up the presentation. But when her peripheral vision caught sudden movement, she glanced over in time to see CherylAnn throw herself into Travis's arms.

Her body stiffened until she saw the lines between Travis's dark brows. Even though he was smiling, those weren't laugh lines. He gently but firmly pushed CherylAnn away.

Becca clutched her buckle box even tighter as she recognized the emotion stabbing through her. She was jealous.

No! It wasn't possible. She didn't care who crawled all over Travis Eden. It was a sure bet *she* didn't want to.

Why was it so hard for her to remember

this man was a rodeo cowboy?

Seconds later he was at her side once again. The announcers finished their jawing, and the crowd began to break up. Some headed for the exit, some for the bar.

Travis leaned down, settling a hand at her waist. "It's almost midnight. You ready to head back to the hotel?"

Becca tried to ignore the small shock of pleasure his warm hand sent radiating through her, but she couldn't keep the image of "crawling all over him" out of her mind. Not trusting her voice, she merely nodded.

It took half an hour for them to work their way through the crowd. They were stopped every few minutes for fans or other contestants to congratulate Travis. Winning two events at the National Finals didn't happen every day.

Since Becca was with him and had also won her event, she was included in the congratulations. She knew a lot of the people they talked to from her year on the circuit, but not nearly as well as Travis knew them. He spoke to each of them with an easy camaraderie. Almost like family.

But then, they were his family. Probably more important to him than his own.

Heaven knew he spent more time with these people. He probably didn't spend a week out of the year at the Garden with Hank and Alex. He had rodeo in his blood. He was a "down the road" kind of man, just like her father. How could she possibly be attracted to a man who could do to her what her father did to her mother?

She wasn't. No way. She wouldn't allow herself to be.

The door was in sight when a group of older cowboys she didn't know stopped Travis. They drew him into their little circle, leaving her standing by herself.

Stifling a yawn, Becca glanced longingly at the door. She'd get to the hotel a lot faster if she caught a cab. She looked back at Travis, who laughed at something one of the men said. What would he do if she just left? What could he do? He didn't have any say in —

"Howdy, sweet thing," a voice whispered next to her ear while a hand snaked across her bottom.

Gagging on beer fumes, she shoved at the strong arm. "Wade Jones, you let go of me."

"Come on, honey. Let's you and me go find us a nice quiet place and have a drink."

Becca was getting mighty tired of fighting off this particular group of cowboys. She couldn't go anywhere without one of them pawing her. "Not for all the gold buckles in the world."

She spun out of his grip and took several strides for the door, but he caught her hand. "Aw, come on. What'll it hurt?"

Her eyes narrowed as she glared at him. "Leave me alone, Wade, or I'll —"

Suddenly a hand gripped Wade's wrist. Travis's voice was low and deadly. "You manhandling my woman, Jones?"

"*Your* woman?"

Becca and Wade asked the question in unison.

Their combined shock allowed Travis to break Wade's grip on Becca's hand. He shoved the cowboy away and drew Becca against him.

She gaped up at him. "What the heck are you —"

"Go along with me," he whispered against her hair.

"But —"

"Since when were you two a couple?" Wade asked belligerently.

"Since I said so," Travis told him. "And you know I protect what's mine, don't you?"

The flash of fear in Wade's red-rimmed eyes told Travis his fellow bull rider remembered the time he caught Wade spooking his horse.

Wade's watery gaze slid away. "Hell, she ain't worth fighting over."

Travis wondered if Wade was talking about Becca or that mare. Either way, he felt the same. "I disagree, but I'm glad you think so."

"Travis?" Becca said in a too-sweet, singsong voice.

"In a minute, darlin'." He pulled her close to head off her tirade until they got outside. "Why don't you go sleep it off, Wade? The way you rode tonight, you need all the help you can get."

Wade slithered into the crowd, casting angry glances back at them.

Travis watched him, then turned to find Becca glaring at him.

He'd hoped he'd be able to discuss his plan with her before this trouble came up again. "Let me explain."

"Let go of me," she said in a withering whisper.

"Not until you promise to listen."

The next thing he felt was a stabbing pain where she crashed the heel of her boot on his instep. He let go of her involuntarily, and she spun toward the door.

"Becca, wait!"

"Go to hell, Travis Eden."

She strode quickly toward the door, but even hobbling, his strides were longer, and he caught up with her just outside. He grabbed her arm. "Will you please stop?"

In answer, she whistled loudly at a cab.

"You're not getting in that cab. You're riding with me."

She glared at him. "I wouldn't ride to the Pearly Gates with you."

He threw the hand that wasn't holding his buckle boxes in the air. "Will you just listen to me?"

The cab slid to the curb. Becca reached for the door, but Travis caught her arm. He leaned down to the driver. "Never mind."

"What are you doing?" she asked sharply.

"Please, Becca, I need to explain."

Another couple got into the cab and it pulled away.

Becca watched it go, then yanked her arm free of his grip. "I'm not —"

"Can we go someplace we aren't a sideshow?" He nodded toward the door. There weren't as many people outside the hotel as inside, but the ones waiting for transportation watched them with avid interest.

Becca looked around and briskly straightened her jacket. "Where?"

"Might as well go on to the truck and head back to the hotel."

She took a moment to consider his suggestion, then said quietly, "I'm not your woman."

"Don't you think I know that?"

"Then why did you tell Wade I am?"

"To protect you."

"What?"

"I'll explain in a minute. Come on."

He led the way to his truck. When he opened the passenger door and offered to help Becca up onto the leather bucket seat, she ignored his hand.

He was damned if he was going to let her ignore him. He clearly remembered how warmly she'd returned his hug when they met backstage after the first go-round. She was not as immune to him as she pretended. Still, he knew he had to tread softly if he was going to get her to cooperate.

"I'm not going to bite," he assured her softly.

She hesitated as she pulled the seat belt across her lap. Then her eyes found his. "Good."

He smiled as she snapped the seat belt in place, then shut the door and came around to slide under the steering wheel.

As he turned east on Flamingo and headed across the Interstate, she said, "Well?"

He threw a glance at her. She sat rigidly in the plush seat. "It's late and there are a lot of drunks in this town, what with casinos giving out free drinks and all. Let me concentrate on getting us to the hotel."

He heard her release a soft sigh, then she relaxed against the seat until he pulled the truck into the Diamond Spurs parking lot. But as soon as he switched off the engine, Becca's hand was on the door latch.

"Wait just a minute."

Becca threw him a wary glance. "You want to talk here?"

Travis's smile faded a notch. Becca acted as if she didn't want anything to do with him. So why did his gut tell him she was more interested than she appeared — or maybe even wanted to be? What would she do if he reached over and traced her bottom lip with his finger? Or his tongue?

Probably bite him.

The thought did not deter certain parts from stirring that had no business coming to life. He shifted on the seat and cleared the fog from his throat. “If we go upstairs, we might disturb your mother.”

She hesitated before letting go of the latch. Then instead of looking at him, she stared out the windshield, her slender fingers absently tracing the outline of her buckle box. “I don’t need your protection, Travis. I’ve been doing fine on my own for fifteen years. I’m not the little girl you once knew, and I’m certainly not your woman.”

At least her anger was gone. Becca always had a quick temper, then was quick to cool off. He credited the trait to her red hair. “Maybe you don’t need my protection, but I need yours.”

Her head snapped around. “You need *my* protection?”

He nodded. “CherylAnn Barnes has been cornering me every chance she gets. She’s dead set on getting me back, or so she says. Didn’t you see her when I stepped off the stage?”

Becca nodded, then smiled wryly. “You want me to beat her up?”

Travis grinned at the image. “That might be fun to watch, but no. CherylAnn’s got at least twenty pounds on you, and about a hundred pounds more of meanness. What I want you to do is be my woman.”

Her answer was quick. "No."

"Just until the Finals are over."

She stared at him a long moment. "You're crazy."

He straightened and leaned a little closer. "Maybe, but think of the advantages, both to you and to me. If everyone thinks we're serious, CherylAnn will look ridiculous chasing me. She'll have to back off."

"What advantage is there for me?"

"Chance and Wade and the others will leave you alone if they think you're mine. They've learned the hard way I don't tolerate any shenanigans when it comes to what's mine. That would go triple for my woman."

Becca leaned against the door, stupefied. "I can't believe I'm hearing this."

"I know it seems a little loco . . ."

"You can say that again!"

"Hey, it worked tonight, didn't it? And the other night at the reception."

"But you — I don't — What —" None of Becca's objections seemed to fit. "Let me get this straight. You want me to pretend to like you just so a few cowboys will quit hitting on me? Don't you think that's a little extreme? A few well-placed slaps will do the same job."

"Don't bet on . . ." Travis trailed off as if he were about to say something he shouldn't.

"Why not?" she probed. "What do you know that I don't?"

"Let me just say that you've become a challenge to them. You've turned all of them down so often, they've become determined to . . . how did they put it? Oh yes. They want to melt your icicles."

Becca's eyes widened. "They told you this?"

"In those exact words."

"Oh." Becca thought back over the times she'd been caught behind the chutes or pulled into an empty pen by one of six or seven cowboys. Now that she thought about it, there did seem to be a pattern, a certain grim determination. So far she'd been able to escape after an elbow punch or a swift kick to the groin, but what if that didn't work? "You don't think they'd resort to force, do you?"

"I don't like to think so," he said, his voice even deeper than usual. "But . . . hell, if they were drunk enough, who knows?"

She tried to swallow the lump that was rapidly forming in her throat, but it came right back. "That's despicable."

"Yeah." He scooted a shade closer and reached over to cover the hands she'd clenched in her lap. "Now you see why I suggested this."

Becca looked down. His huge hand swallowed both of hers easily. His fingers felt warm surrounding hers, comforting. The fact that he wanted to help her made the warmth creep up her arms all the way to her heart.

She tried to push the feeling away, knowing she was vulnerable. Though her mother had been there physically, during the past year Becca had done everything — from cooking their breakfast in the morning to driving the long miles from rodeo to rodeo. She'd been virtually on her own so long that anyone who showed her the slightest bit of kindness made her tear up.

That's all this emotion was. It certainly wasn't any special feeling for this rodeo cowboy.

"What do you say?" he pressed.

Becca studied Travis's face. Though the parking lot was well lit, his hat threw shadows across his features, making them seem rough-hewn. "I can't believe you're serious."

"Why not? It's perfect. We both get some

relief from unwanted attention so we can concentrate on what we came to do — win gold buckles."

He was good, she had to give him that. He knew exactly the buttons to push. Did he know she had to win the championship . . . and why?

No. They hadn't told Hank or Alex or anyone else their troubles.

She stared blindly out the window as she considered his scheme. On the one hand, it would be nice to be able to concentrate on winning the championship. On the other, she'd have to spend even more time with Travis, which shattered her concentration all to pieces.

"You don't have to do this, Travis," she said quietly. "You've already done so much for us. I can handle these cowboys if I'm careful."

"Then do it for me. I want CherylAnn off my back." He paused, his hand tightening over hers. "Think of it as just another way to repay me."

Becca's gaze fell to their hands. The final button. She owed this man more than she could ever repay, debts accrued from the day she was born. "What, exactly, would I have to do?"

"Instead of acting like you can't stand

the sight of me, you need to act like you like me."

His words slapped her in the face. She didn't realize she'd been that obvious. She'd just been trying to protect herself from liking him too much.

She searched his shadowed face in the dim light. Though his million-dollar smile curled his lips, it seemed tight. With what? Anxiety? Determination? It looked downright artificial.

For the second time she was struck with the notion that he used his smile as a mask. She wanted to know — with keen desperation — what his mask covered.

From the moment he'd stopped along the highway, she'd sensed an undercurrent of emotion in him. Something she couldn't quite put her finger on. She wanted to know what made Travis Eden tick, what lay beneath the always smiling, good ol' cowboy exterior. She had the feeling no one else in the world had an inkling.

How was that possible when the whole world knew Travis Eden? At least, the rodeo world, which was millions of people.

Yet, she'd bet Cocoa that no one knew the real Travis Eden.

"Would pretending to like me be so hard?" he asked quietly.

Hard? No. The hard part had been acting like she didn't. But if she was going to unravel the mystery that was Travis Eden, she had to agree to his plan. Which meant letting down her guard. Which wasn't smart.

Yet how could she say no? She owed him so much. Besides, for some strange reason, she wanted to help him.

"I guess I could manage."

His hand shifted so their fingers were laced, and without moving perceptibly, his whole body relaxed. "Good."

Becca tried to ignore the intimacy of their entwined fingers, the warmth of his palm against hers. "Are we . . ." She cleared her throat. "Are we going to tell anyone we're faking it? Like our families?"

He considered her question, then said, "Better not. The more people we convince, the more likely we'll succeed."

"I don't like keeping secrets from my mother, especially one like this. She's been after me to find a nice young man to settle down with. She thinks I need someone to take care of me after . . ." She trailed off, realizing what she'd almost told him. Somehow Travis made her forget there were secrets she wasn't supposed to tell.

"After what?"

Becca shook her head. "What about after the Finals? If my mother, Hank and Alex think we're . . . dating, it might be awkward when we no longer are. We're neighbors now, you know."

"Yes, I know." His eyes slid away. "Why don't we let that take care of itself? We can always tell them afterward."

"Just don't go getting any ideas that this is permanent. Nothing personal, but I'm not going to spend my life with a rodeo cowboy."

His eyes narrowed. "What's wrong with rodeo cowboys?"

"They're never around when you need them." When he started to comment, she hurried on, "But let's get back to the subject, okay?"

He raised a brow but didn't press the issue. "Don't worry. I have plans of my own. The last thing I need right now is a wife."

His words reinforced her certainty that instead of blood, Travis had gasoline running in his veins. At least enough to get him to the next rodeo. She pulled her hand away. "Good. Then it's settled. We start tomorrow."

He stared at her a long time, his eyes looking as if a battle were being waged behind them. Finally, his voice deeper than usual, he said, "We'll start right now."

"Now? What can we do now?"

But he'd already climbed out of the truck. A few seconds later her door opened. Instead of letting her step down, he caught her around the waist and lifted her out. Surprised, her gaze found his. His eyes held hers as he slid her slowly along his body until her feet reached the pavement.

"We're going to seal our bargain with a kiss." His voice was husky. "We need the practice."

Becca's eyes fell to his wide, sensuous mouth. Her curves molded to the hard, warm planes of his frame. Shivers of anticipation raced along her skin, making every hair stand at attention. Suddenly her desire to know him became physical. She wanted to slide her fingers into his hair, to taste him, to brand his scent on her brain.

She barely summoned enough strength to shake her head dazedly. "No public displays of affection allowed."

"Wrong. Couples touch each other. If we're going to make this work, you have to remember that and act accordingly." His head lowered fractionally with each word until the brim of his hat pushed hers off. "I'm going to be holding your hand, putting my arm around you, kissing you. Might as well get used to it now. . . ."

Chapter Five

An instant before Travis's lips touched Becca's, he heard her utter his name. Half protest, half moan, the sound inflamed him. The kiss he'd intended as a controlled, precise effort, meant to break down her resistance, immediately changed into something else entirely.

The alarm bells clanging in his head were drowned out by the warmth of her lips sending thunderbolts through his body, incinerating rational thought, melting control. Blood hammered through his brain, drowning every sound but her tiny whimpers, his own harsh breathing.

When she leaned into him for support, wrapping her arms around his neck, he groaned and shifted his legs so she stood between his thighs. His last lucid thought was concern that the growing evidence of his desire would frighten her. But instead of pulling away, a shudder ran from her lips to the knees intertwined with his. He felt every bump and shiver along the way.

He emitted a groan that came all the way from his gut and backed her up against his truck. His tongue traced the outline of her mouth, then coaxed her lips apart to slip inside. When her tongue met his without hesitation, he ground his hips into hers. They moaned together.

A car passed behind the truck, seeking a parking spot.

"Damn." Ice water doused Travis, cutting the edge of his desire enough for him to lift his head. What the hell was he doing?

"What's wrong?" she asked, still leaning on his support.

"Nothing. I just never dreamed you'd — Damn."

Her eyes opened, still smoldering with passion. Her lips were swollen from the violence of his kiss. It took a Herculean effort to keep his head from dipping to taste them again.

"Where did you learn to kiss like that?" he asked in a voice still deep and heavy with desire.

Her eyes cleared suddenly and widened with the same amazement he felt at the intense heat generated by the mere touch of their lips.

She dropped her forehead to his shoulder. "Damn you. That's not the kind of kiss we'll give each other in public."

No, it wasn't. And if he were smart, they wouldn't be giving each other any more of them in private.

So why the sudden, overwhelming desire to be stupid?

He gently lifted her chin. "Don't hide from me, darlin'."

Confusion filled her blue eyes. "Maybe this isn't such a —"

"It's late." He straightened, not wanting to give her a chance to change her mind. "We'd better get some sleep or we'll be exhausted tomorrow."

Travis locked his truck, retrieved Becca's hat, then escorted her into the hotel with a hand on her waist. Even though it was after two, he saw several people he knew feeding coins into slot machines. He nodded as he and Becca passed, his smile tightening at the speculative looks thrown their way. Word that they'd come in so late, arm in arm, would be all over the rodeo crowd by tomorrow.

Even though it was what he wanted, Travis brought Becca closer, as if he could protect her from the curious eyes.

They didn't say a word until they reached the suite. Becca had her key out of her pocket before he could even remember where he'd put his, but when she tried to slip the card into the slot her hand shook.

He steadied her hand with his.

"Thanks," she murmured as she turned the door latch.

Somehow it felt natural to enter the suite with Becca. Like he was coming home.

She quickly turned toward her room. "Good night."

He caught her hand. When she lifted her face to see what he wanted, he kissed her mouth again, quickly. It wasn't like the kiss in the parking lot, but still sent tiny waves of electricity crackling along his spine.

"I've got appearances in the morning," he said quietly. "I'll meet you back here at noon and take you and your mother to lunch."

Her eyes were huge. "Why?"

"We need to be seen together." He squeezed her hand. "And get to know one another again. People will be asking questions. We need to know the answers."

"Are you sure this is smart?"

"No. But do you have a better idea?"

Her eyes searched his. "All right. I'll

meet you here at noon."

Her lips were still slightly swollen, and her cheeks were flushed a bright pink. Her musky scent curled around his brain, driving desire deep into his gut. He wanted to pick her up, toss her onto his king-size bed and make love to her for the rest of the night.

The violence of his passion startled him. He'd never reacted so intensely to a woman. Ever.

He couldn't afford to let desire get the better of him with this one. She'd made it clear she would never consider him as a potential mate. Even if she would, he wasn't ready for marriage. First he needed time alone at the Circle E to slow down, to heal, to learn who the hell he was.

With a garbled, "Good night," he spun on his heel and retreated to his room.

Saturday, Go-Round #2

Travis let himself into the suite, flexing his right hand to work out the kinks from signing so many autographs. He must've signed hundreds — hats, shirts, NFR programs, tickets. A couple of giggling high school girls even wanted him to sign their stomachs. He'd compromised by signing the backs of their hands.

He used to love this kind of thing, but today he'd wanted to ask these people if they didn't have anything better to do with their lives than wait a couple of hours just for the signature of some old cowpoke.

He reckoned he should be grateful for their interest. It paid for this fancy suite. But somehow he couldn't sum up a single bit of appreciation. He just wanted to get the hell out of there.

All morning he'd looked forward to his afternoon with the Larsons. Though it didn't make any sense, being with Becca reminded him of wading in Blue Rock Creek, which ran along the boundary between the Circle E and the Garden. The cold water always got his blood going, but at the same time the sound of water tripping over rocks soothed his soul.

Travis stepped into the main room of the suite, half-expecting Becca to be waiting for him on one of the chairs or couches. His smile — which had brightened in direct proportion to the number of people he'd talked to — relaxed.

She wasn't there.

His smile faded a notch until he realized she was probably still in her room. He strode over to the door and knocked.

No answer.

Where the hell was she? He told her to meet him there at noon. It was a quarter past. Surely she didn't get mad and leave because he was fifteen minutes late. That didn't sound like Becca.

Concerned, he slowly opened the Larsons' door. The room was dark as pitch, though it was the middle of a sunny day. The air inside felt dead, like a tomb.

He switched on the nearest lamp and stopped cold. Joy Larson lay in the double bed nearest the window, stretched out like a corpse — and just as still.

Travis's smile vanished and with a mumbled curse, he stepped between the beds and switched on another lamp. Joy's hands rested on her stomach. Her face was ghostly white. If she breathed, he couldn't tell.

He placed a finger on her neck and felt a faint but steady pulse, then sank to the edge of the bed in relief.

"Mrs. Larson," he said softly. "Wake up."

No response. Not even an eyelash moved.

He placed a hand over hers and shook gently. "Wake up, Mrs. Larson."

Still no response.

He shook harder, called her louder and louder until he was shouting.

Still no response.

Fear lanced through him. This was no migraine. This woman was gravely ill.

"What are you doing?"

He jerked his head to see Becca framed by the door, a small white paper bag in her hand.

He stood and faced her. "What the hell's going on?"

Becca's gaze slid to her mother's still figure. "What do you mean? She's got a head—"

"Don't lie to me. Your mother's either in a coma or on drugs so major they cause the next best thing."

Becca searched his eyes for a long moment, then glanced down at the bag in her hand. She walked slowly over to the dresser, placed the bag on top and reached inside.

"Becca," he said.

She held out a small bottle.

He took it from her, but the name of the drug didn't mean anything. He couldn't remember the last time he'd taken anything stronger than aspirin. "What is it?"

"A painkiller." The eyes she lifted to his

were huge, somber. "The strongest thing you can get this side of morphine."

Once again fear stabbed him. "What's wrong with her?"

She gestured to the door. "Let's talk out there. I know it doesn't seem like talking can disturb her, but she rests easier when it's quiet."

He set the bottle on the dresser, then followed Becca into the living room, quietly closing the bedroom door behind him.

She pushed herself into a corner of the plushest couch, folding her knees against her chest and wrapping both arms around them.

Travis sat beside her on the edge of the soft cushion, his back rigid. "What's wrong with her? Don't start with the headaches again. I've known people with migraines. They were never like this."

"Momma has — She's —" Pain flashed across Becca's heart-shaped face, and she turned to stare out the windows. "It's hard to talk about. We haven't told anyone."

He placed a comforting hand on her crossed arms. "I'm not just anyone. Am I, monkey-face?"

Her anguished gaze returned to his. Tears made her blue eyes pale. "Momma's dying."

Every muscle in Travis's body froze. Though the thought had crossed his mind when he found Joy in bed, he hadn't really believed it. He didn't want to believe it now. "Are you sure?"

Becca nodded jerkily. "She has a brain tumor. That's why she has the headaches."

Travis stood abruptly, as if he could escape her words. Whirling, he strode around the couch to the bank of windows looking up the Strip — gaudy as always, and full of life. He wanted to pick up the couch and hurl it through the glass. "Can't they operate?"

"No. If they did, they'd kill her." The quiet misery of something long ago accepted shaded her voice. "Even if they could operate, it would cost more than I could make if I won every rodeo for five years."

"How many doctors did you see?" he demanded.

"Two. Both of them said the same thing."

"Where were they?"

"One was in Paris, Texas, where we lived for several years. The other in Dallas."

"Were they experts?"

"The one in Dallas was."

He shook his head. "Not good enough."

She stood and faced him. "What do you mean, 'not good enough'?"

"I mean that one guy's opinion could be wrong. We've got to find the best brain surgeon in the country."

"Don't you think I wanted to do that two years ago when we found out? We can't afford the kind of medical care she needs."

He straightened, the panic receding as possibilities opened up. "I can. Claire's been taking the winnings and sponsorship money that I don't need to live off of and investing it for me. I've got more than I can —"

"No!" Becca chopped the air with her hands. "I don't accept charity."

His eyes narrowed. "Not even to save your mother's life?"

She flinched as if he'd slapped her. "That's not fair. You don't know what I've gone through the past two years. You don't know the pain she's suffered. I've done everything the doctors said could be done for her, and more besides."

He stepped closer, until only the couch separated them. He wanted to reach across the plush expanse, drag her into his arms and assure her he'd take care of everything. "You're right. I don't know what you've gone through, because I didn't keep up with you. I'm sorry for that, more than you know. But two years is a long time in medicine. New discoveries are made all the time. We can find out who's the best brain doctor in the world and take her there next week."

She crossed her arms over her stomach. "She's my mother, Travis, not yours. It's not your problem."

Her words hit him right between the eyes. Joy Larson *wasn't* his mother. So why was her imminent death tearing him apart?

He felt the same way he felt fifteen years ago, when the Larsons vanished from his life. Their leaving — and the way they left — ripped him in two. They'd been part of his family all his life. Hell, they *were* his family those last few years, after his parents died. Hank sure didn't have time for him. But Joy and Becca had needed him, believed in him as a man, which at that point in his life was exactly what he'd needed.

Mrs. Larson had taken the place of his mother. That's why he was so upset. Losing Joy the first time was like losing his own mother all over again. Now that he'd found her again, he wasn't about to lose her. Not without one hell of a fight.

He locked gazes with Becca. "I'm making it my problem."

She looked at him as if he'd grown horns. "What part of 'no' don't you understand? I told you, we don't —"

"Take charity," he spat. "So you'd rather she died?"

His intentionally harsh question made her explode. She yanked up a pillow and threw it at him. "Don't you dare tell me what I feel! You don't understand anything."

He deflected the pillow easily. "What's the harm in getting a third opinion?"

"We can't afford it. We have . . . other expenses now."

"I can afford it."

"How can I make you understand? The doctors said she probably wouldn't survive an operation. There's only a twenty-percent chance of success." Her anger deflated suddenly. Tears streaming down her cheeks, she sank hard onto the coffee table and buried her face in her hands. "At least now I'll have her a few more months, maybe even another year. If they operate, I'll lose her. And then I'll have nothing. No one."

Her grief made Travis feel like an invisible hand had grabbed his heart and squeezed. He knew her pain because it echoed his own, but her grief far outshadowed his. She was Joy Larson's daughter, and there wasn't a fifteen-year gap in their relationship.

Four long strides took him around the couch. He dropped onto the coffee table and gathered Becca in his arms. She struggled for a second, then buried her face against his shoulder and cried.

As he held her, his first instinct was to tell her she'd always have him, but that wasn't true. He wouldn't be any good to anyone until he'd spent time alone on Yellow Jack Mountain. He had to heal himself before he could help anyone else.

So he just held her, wishing he could absorb her pain.

As he waited for her tears to subside, he became determined to find a doctor who could help the woman who'd helped him when he needed it most. He knew it wasn't just for Joy. He wanted to do it for Becca. He wanted to see her smile again and he wanted to know he was the one who put the smile on her face.

The strength of that desire confused him.

To avoid the confusion, he thought

about how to carry out his plan.

His best bet was his new brother-in-law, Jake Anderson. Claire mentioned he was on the board of several hospitals. Surely he'd know where to start asking. Jake and Claire would be in Las Vegas later in the week. He'd discuss Joy's condition with Jake then.

As Becca began to calm, Travis concentrated on her. More than anything he wanted to lift her mouth to his, to finish what they'd started the night before. But she didn't need his passion right now.

Funny, if he thought of Joy Larson almost as a mother, then logic would make Becca his sister. Yet his feelings for the woman in his arms were anything but brotherly.

At last only soft hiccups remained.

"I'm sorry," Becca said quietly. "I didn't mean to cry all over you."

"Don't you remember, monkey-face? You always came to me when you were sad."

She slowly wrapped her arms around his waist. "Thank you. It's been a long time since . . ."

He rubbed a hand down the column of her spine. "Since what?"

"Nothing." She shook her head as she

lifted it. "Please don't tell anyone about Momma. She doesn't want to be an object of pity. And if the media find out, no telling what they'll make of it."

"I won't tell anyone outside the family," he promised.

"But —"

"You can trust them." He brushed aside a red curl glued to her cheek by tears. "Hank could put a clam to shame, and Alex won't tell anyone if we ask her not to. Besides, they'd find out eventually. You won't be able to keep her condition a secret living so close together here."

She frowned. "All right, but nobody else."

He placed a gentle kiss on her temple. "Not another soul. Trust me, okay?"

She searched his eyes, then sighed heavily. "I shouldn't. I don't know you anymore. Yet somehow I do trust you."

Her statement unraveled a knot deep inside him. "You do know me, monkey-face. I'm the same as I always was. Just an old cowboy."

Her frown deepened, and he thought for a minute she'd pull away. Instead, after a brief hesitation, she leaned back against him.

"Now you know why I have to win the

championship," she said softly. "I need the money for the Circle E."

The hand traveling up her back froze. "What do you mean?"

"Momma never gave up on the idea of going home, even though we barely made enough to feed and clothe ourselves. When we learned she was dying, I knew I had to take her back. She was born on the Circle E, and loves it I think as much as she loves me. I knew —" she swallowed hard "— I knew she'd be much happier if she could spend her last days there."

A knife plunged deep into Travis's heart, then twisted. The land he wanted, the mountains that would make him whole, had just been snatched out of reach. There's no way Becca would sell him the ranch, even if he was enough of a sidewinder to ask her to.

The only way he'd get the ranch was if she lost it — which she would if she didn't win the championship. And rookies rarely won.

A brief flicker of hope flared through him, but he violently stamped it out. He wouldn't be able to live with himself if he profited from their loss. In fact, he had to help her win the championship — now more than ever.

What would he do if he couldn't have the Circle E?

The wounds of a lifetime, the open sores on his soul, cried out for the vistas of the timbered mountains that formed a small section of the Great Divide. The land he'd yearned for all his life.

Why? The Circle E wasn't the only ranch for sale. There were other mountains, other vistas. Hank had been telling him so for years. Why was it the Circle E or nothing?

Because it was home. Because that's where he grew up and became a man. Because that's where he'd been loved — by Becca and her mother.

Amazed by the sudden insight, he instinctively tightened his hold on Becca.

How had he ever allowed himself to lose track of these two women? Why hadn't he sought them out as soon as he was old enough? How could he have let their love slip away from him?

After the Larsons left, he threw himself into bull riding, finding a ride to a rodeo nearly every weekend. It didn't matter where the rodeo was, as long as he could get away from the Garden. He left to pursue bull riding full-time the day after he graduated from high school and got caught up in rodeo's down-the-road kind of life. The love of a woman old enough to be his mother and a girl younger than his sister didn't mean much to a rambling rodeo cowboy. Or so he'd told himself.

How could he have been so stupid?

And what the hell was he going to do now?

"Travis?"

He brought his thoughts back to the woman in his arms. "What, monkey-face?"

She pulled back and gazed up at him. "Thank you for letting me cry on your shoulder."

He settled his smile back on his face. "Two thank-yous in one day? We're setting some kind of record here."

Her red brows came together, then she wiped her thumb across his mouth. "You don't have to smile for me, Travis. I like you better without your million-dollar mask."

His smile disappeared. Mask? He'd never thought of his smile that way, but she was right. The more nervous or angry or frustrated he felt, the bigger his smile.

How could she know him so well? It was as if she could see into his soul.

What else did she see there?

He shuddered at the thought.

She laid a hand on his cheek. "Are you okay?"

He studied her heart-shaped face. Her eyes, nose and cheeks were red from crying. He'd never seen features more beautiful. Part of him wanted to drag her down on the couch and make love to her the rest of his life. Another part wanted to run screaming from the room.

Okay? How could he be okay when he didn't know what he needed, what he wanted or who the hell he was?

Chapter Six

Sunday, Go-Round #3

Becca came awake slowly, aware at first only of the pain in her left knee. Trying to beat CherylAnn's time of fourteen point two zero seconds in the second round last night, she'd rated Cocoa a hair too soon, causing the mare to slice the barrel. Becca was able to keep the barrel from tipping over, saving herself from a five-second penalty, but her knee had slammed into the oversize Coors can.

That, added to all the dancing she'd done at the buckle presentation afterward, made her knee pulse with pain.

Rolling to her side, she rubbed it as she opened her eyes. The first thing she noticed was her mother's empty bed.

The headache must finally be gone.

Her own pain forgotten in her relief, Becca threw off her covers. "Momma? Where are you?"

Only quiet answered her.

Getting up, she tossed wild curls out of her face and limped over to the bathroom, which was dark and empty. Becca finally found her mother on the plushest chair in the suite's living room with her sewing in her lap. On her good days, Joy sewed the beautiful shirts Becca wore in the arena.

"There you are." Still dressed in the T-shirt she slept in, Becca walked over and pressed a kiss on her mother's cheek. "How are you feeling?"

The smile Joy gave her was weak, but at least it was a smile. "Much better, dear."

Becca sank to the square coffee table in front of her mother's chair. "What time did you get up? Why didn't you wake me?"

Her mother glanced down at her sewing. "I woke up around four, but didn't get out of bed until six. I didn't want to wake you that early. Travis said you didn't get in until two."

The knowing smile on her mother's face made Becca want to groan. He obviously said something about their "relationship" to her mother. The thought made her frown. She wished he had let her tell her mother in her own way. She didn't want Joy's hopes raised so that she'd be crushed when she realized Becca and Travis were just pretending to be dating. “Yes, we went to the buckle presentation again.”

“Did you win another buckle?” Joy asked.

Becca shook her head. “Cocoa sliced the second barrel. I was a full second off the lead, which wasn’t even in the money.” She made a face. “CherylAnn Barnes placed first. You should’ve seen her gloat afterward.”

“Did Travis get a buckle last night?”

“No. He placed second in bull riding and fourth in team roping.” Even though neither of them placed first, Travis had insisted they go to the buckle presentation so they could be seen together as a “couple.”

“He’s such a nice young man,” Joy said blandly.

Right. It was nice of him to insist she dance every dance after injuring her knee. Although, to be fair, she’d told him she wasn’t hurt. “I guess so.”

“He seems right taken with you.” Her mother smiled as she bit off a length of thread.

Since her mother wasn’t looking, Becca rolled her eyes. Trust Travis to pour it on thick. Becca was definitely not in the mood to get into this discussion. “I’m hungry.

What time is it?" She leaned back to see the clock on the wall in the kitchenette. "Eleven? Dang, I slept late. Travis wanted me to be ready at noon in case Hank and Alex make it in early. And I wanted to ice my knee."

Joy glanced down at her daughter's bare knees. "That's a nasty bruise. Did you hit a barrel?"

She grimaced. "I barely kept it from tipping, which is a good thing or I would've kissed the championship goodbye."

"Have you heard anything about the truck?"

Becca nodded. "I talked to Mr. Pruitt yesterday. Since the truck's so old, he had to order a new radiator from Los Angeles. He thinks it'll be ready Thursday or Friday."

"That's good."

Becca supposed it didn't matter when she got the truck. Travis would still insist on driving her everywhere. "Are you hungry?"

Joy pointed her threaded needle at the table. "No. Travis ordered a big breakfast for us this morning. He and I had a nice talk over coffee. There's plenty left for you. You can warm it up in the microwave."

Frowning, Becca limped over to the

huge table with ten padded chairs. Several covered dishes were spread across the end closest to the kitchenette. Picking them up one by one, she found bacon, sausage, scrambled eggs and biscuits. The same things she'd found waiting for her when she wakened the last two days.

The meal was nothing out of the ordinary, but it was the thought behind it that bothered her. Ever since she'd agreed to be Travis's "woman," he'd taken over her life. He'd paid for every meal, taken her everywhere she needed to go, done exactly the right thing every step of the way.

The problem was, she was beginning to like it. She liked not having to drive everywhere. She liked not making every little decision of the day — from where to go for lunch to what to do after the rodeo. She even liked the feel of his hand holding hers, his strong arm circling her waist, his lips settling over hers. . . .

The lid to the biscuit plate rattled loudly as she dropped it.

This wasn't good. It was downright stupid. She couldn't let herself get used to anything to do with Travis Eden. She especially couldn't let herself begin to believe any of this was real. The only reason he was doing any of it was to stay clear of

CherylAnn Barnes. To him, Becca was "monkey-face." And that was all.

Besides, he was a *rodeo cowboy*. The National Finals were probably the longest he ever stayed in one place, and only because he had to be there for ten go-rounds. She didn't want a man who was here today, gone this afternoon.

Maybe she should call off their little game. The more time she spent with him, the more she was in danger of —

She halted her thought abruptly. She wasn't about to say "falling in love," was she?

Uh-uh. No way. Not with a rodeo cowboy.

Suddenly the door opened with a loud click and the object of her thoughts entered. His smile relaxed when he saw her. "Finally up?"

He walked the few paces to where she stood and bent to kiss her. Just before he made contact, she put her hand between their mouths. "Momma's up."

His gaze cut to where her mother was busying herself with sewing. Then he raised a brow and lowered his voice. "We need to convince her, too, you know."

She backed up. "I . . . haven't brushed my teeth yet."

As she retreated, he drew a bead down her frame. "Not exactly Victoria's Secret, but I won't complain."

She'd forgotten she was still in her sleeping shirt, which barely covered the essentials. Heat stung her cheeks — but it didn't come from embarrassment. The fever burning through her veins came from the depths of his hot blue eyes.

He stepped closer. "Keep looking at me like that, darlin', and I'll forget your mother's right behind me."

With a tiny gasp, she turned to escape into her room. As she did she bumped her knee against a chair and yelped.

He caught her shoulders, then bent and lifted her left knee from the shadows behind the table. His narrowed eyes met hers. "You told me you didn't hurt yourself when you hit that barrel."

In order to keep her balance, she had to grab his shoulders. "You said we needed to dance."

He glared at her. "Damn it, Becca. I didn't know you were hurt."

"It's just a bruise."

"Right. And this is just another rodeo."

Her gaze slid away from his. "Can I have my knee back, please?"

His large hands released her as gently as

he'd held her. "Go sit over by your momma. I'll get you some ice."

"I can get my own ice."

The stare he gave her was granite.

"Okay, okay." She rolled her eyes as she turned toward her door.

His arm shot out to keep her door from opening. "Where do you think you're going?"

"I'm going in to put some clothes on while you get the ice."

His face relaxed into a sexy smile. "What for? I've already seen everything there is to see with this outfit, and I kinda like the view."

"Tough toenails, cowboy," she muttered, then chopped at his elbow and yanked open her door.

Monday, Go-Round #4

"Uncle Travis! We're here!"

Becca smiled at the animated face pressed against the back window of the blue crew cab. Hank had barely come to a stop at the edge of the corral when Matt threw the door open and launched himself at Travis.

Travis caught him easily and threw him, laughing, high in the air.

"Unca Travis! Me, too!" Sarah waved frantically from her car seat.

"Just a minute, cricket." Travis settled Matt on the ground and reached for the front passenger door. "Let's see if your mom is still sane after a night and day in the car with you guys."

As Travis opened the door for Alex, Becca hesitantly approached the back door where Sarah fought against the buckles. "Can I help you out?"

Sarah raised eyes just like her uncle's and reached her hands out to Becca. "I'm stuck!"

Smiling, Becca stepped up onto the running board. She could see why Sarah hadn't been able to undo the buckle herself. The latch release took two strong hands.

"We got the strongest buckle on the market," Hank explained from the driver's seat. "Otherwise Sarah would be out as soon as we put her in."

"It's good to see you again, Becca." Alex climbed down from the truck with Travis's assistance. "Thanks for coming out to help."

"You're very welcome." She grimaced as she finally sprang Sarah from her prison. "There."

Sarah giggled with pleasure and wiggled out of her car seat. She threw her chubby arms around Becca's neck. "Thank you."

Touched by the little girl's freely given affection, Becca hugged her back. "You're welcome, sweetheart."

"See my new boots?" Sarah thrust one foot forward. "Unca Jake gave them to me, and it wasn't even Christmas."

Becca stroked the blue and white snowflake design. "I know. You showed them to me last week. How do you keep them so beautiful?"

"Momma won't let me wear them except —"

"Bet ya can't catch me, bugface," Matt cried at his sister.

Her boots forgotten in the heat of challenge, Sarah scrambled out of the truck and raced after Matt and J.J. "Oh yes, I can, turkey breath!"

Before Becca could step down, two strong hands caught her around the waist and lifted her to the ground. She emitted a startled gasp, then frowned up at Travis. He wasn't wasting a single minute before establishing his claim over her in front of Hank and Alex.

He rested his arm across her shoulders as he asked Alex, "How was the trip?"

Alex glanced between them speculatively, but with a big smile. "With my three kids, how do you think it was?"

"Where's Leon?" Hank asked as he came around the truck.

"He had some business in town," Travis answered. "He said to go ahead and unload. How many did you end up bringing?"

Hank returned his brother's gaze steadily. "Got a ten-horse trailer. How many do you think I brought?"

Travis grinned. "Ten."

Hank nodded curtly. "Leon want us to put them in the usual place?"

Travis nodded.

Hank whistled loudly. "J.J.! Come get Bandit out of the trailer."

"Is Bandit J.J.'s?" Becca asked Travis as they started toward the long trailer.

He shook his head. "Bandit's one of the best roping horses I've ever seen, but he's an ornery cuss when it comes to loading and unloading. It's the damnedest thing. With J.J., he's as gentle as a lamb. I have yet to see a horse — green or broke — that J.J. can't handle."

J.J. quickly left the game of tag to help his father while Alex corralled the two younger children at a safe distance.

During the next half hour Becca helped the Eden men unload the ten specially trained rodeo horses into the extra barn at Leon Whitehead's ranch. Hank used the ranch, which was twenty minutes southeast of Las Vegas, to stable the award-winning horses he and his men trained throughout the year.

As J.J. led the last one into a stall, Becca stopped beside Hank, who was getting a drink of water from a hose. "All these are roping horses?"

Travis came up behind her. "A couple are for bulldogging."

"No barrel racing horses?" she asked the brothers.

"We've never found anyone good enough to train them," Travis said.

Hank straightened and handed the hose to Travis, then he looked Becca dead in the eye. "I've been planning to talk to you about that. I don't know what your plans are during the next few years, or what you plan to do when you quit the circuit. Would you be interested in the job when you stop barrel racing full-time?"

Becca blinked in surprise. She'd been worried about how she and her mother were going to live while she got her barrel racing school up and running. A job at the

Garden would be the perfect solution.

Her gaze slid to Travis, who drank deeply from the water. Did he have a hand in this?

"How do you know I'm good enough?" she asked.

"You said you trained Cocoa."

She nodded. "I raised her after her mother died during foaling."

"I watched the broadcast of the first two rounds. She's probably the best-trained horse in the Finals, which means she's one of the best-trained barrel racers in the world."

Though Hank's praise warmed her heart, Becca made a face. "That means the mistakes in the last two performances were my fault."

"Yep."

She was not surprised by his blunt response. She'd learned during the brief stays at the Circle E she and her mother had been able to manage these past few months that he always told the truth, no matter how painful. He said nobody learned anything from false flattery.

She respected his honesty. "When would the job be open?"

"As soon as you've a mind to take it," he said. "You thinking of quitting soon?"

"Maybe this year. Depends on . . ." If she didn't win the championship, she wouldn't be around to work at the Garden. But she didn't want to tell him about her troubles with the loan. Especially with Travis standing there. "On a couple of things. Can I let you know later?"

Becca watched Hank give Travis a questioning glance. Travis shrugged, then his gaze slid away as he looked back at J.J., who was busy giving the horses a healthy helping of sweet feed. Travis's reaction made the hairs on the back of Becca's neck prickle, though she had no idea why.

"Consider it an open offer," Hank said. "And don't worry about me giving the job to anybody else. I'll wait as long as I have to for the best."

She smiled. "Thanks, Hank."

"You ready to head back to town?" Travis placed his hand at her waist. As always, the sudden warmth made her shiver. "We better get going if we're going to clean up before we leave for the arena."

"I'm ready when you are," she told him.

Travis drew a keycard from his shirt pocket and handed it to his brother. "Same suite as last year."

Hank took the card. "Right. We'll be along directly."

* * *

"Travis!"

He barely heard the call above the hubbub of the Gold Coast Dance Hall. Turning, he saw Harriet Bradley waving at him. With four national championships during the early nineteen-eighties, Harriet was one of the best barrel racers of her day, and a good friend.

A glance told Travis Becca was still safely ensconced at a table beside the dance floor, talking with Alex, so he detoured over to Harriet.

"Nice ride, Trav," the older woman said. "You gonna win that eighth gold buckle?"

He grinned. "Anything's possible. You see the barrel racing tonight?"

Harriet patted the chair beside her.

Travis set the three drinks he'd just purchased on the table and sat.

"Becca's beating herself," Harriet said. "I've seen it a thousand times. Too uptight. Too nervous. That horse she's got is the best one out there. The mistakes she's making are mental ones. Becca knows what to do. She just needs to relax enough to do it."

"How can I help?" he asked.

"The best thing you can do for that little gal is to take her mind off running in the

Finals. Give her something to think about besides the next go-round." Harriet poked an elbow in his ribs. "From what I hear, you're working on it. Got a thing for barrel racers, don't ya? Hell, if I were fifteen years younger, I'd give her a run for her money."

Travis laughed and planted a kiss on Harriet's cheek. "If Becca didn't already have her bridle on me, I'd take you up on that threat."

"Get on outta here, you sweet-talkin' cowboy, before my own man decides to check on me."

"Thanks, Harriet. If I can ever do anything for you, just let me know."

"As if you don't help me every year with my rodeo for the local orphanage. But don't worry none about me asking again, Trav. I will."

Travis picked up the drinks and worked his way across the crowded dance hall, receiving congratulations on his latest go-round bull riding win. Halfway to the table, he stopped dead when he saw Becca dragged onto the dance floor by a huge steer wrestler. His gaze followed their progress to the floor as he made a beeline to the table and slapped the drinks down hard.

Alex grabbed his hand as he turned to cut in. "Sit down, Travis. She's okay. Dean is harmless."

"Her knee's hurt," he said. "That's why she's not out there with me."

"Give the guy a break, will you? The men outnumber the women in here four to one. With the way cowboys love to dance, you think any of us will be left alone? I've turned down over a dozen guys myself."

He finally allowed her to pull him onto the chair next to her. "Why? You love to dance."

"I probably would if Hank were here. Since he's not, I don't want anybody to say I'm going behind his back. Besides, I'm tired. I probably should've gone back to the hotel with him and helped put the kids to bed. But he insisted there wasn't room in the truck since Joy was riding with him." She made a face that said her husband didn't fool her one bit.

Travis took a swig of beer. Knowing how little recreation Alex had in her life, Hank gave her every opportunity. Plus, Hank enjoyed time alone with his kids.

The song ended. Travis straightened in time to see Becca's escape from the dance floor foiled by another cowboy. Travis had to get up before his blood started boiling. Setting his beer down, he grabbed his sister-in-law's hand. "You're not too tired to dance with me, are you?"

"How can I refuse the man who taught me to dance?"

Alex's wistful smile barely registered as Travis hauled her onto the dance floor.

After a few circuits where Travis paid more attention to Becca than Alex, his partner said, "You've got it bad, don't you, Travis?"

Startled, he looked down at his brother's wife. "What do you mean?"

"I've never seen you so fired up about a woman, not even CherylAnn." She patted his shoulder. "I'm glad. Becca's more your type."

His smile widened. He hated lying to Alex. She knew him better than anybody except his sister, probably because she knew his brother so well. Though he and Hank didn't seem to have much in common on the surface, deep down they were just alike. If only he could find another woman like Alex — one who cared more about what was inside him than the color of his buckles. "We're not engaged or anything."

"Good. Don't go too fast. Make sure you're as in love with the woman as you are with the ranch."

Travis lost a beat, causing Alex to stumble into him. "Is that what you think I'm doing? Trying to marry Becca so I can have the Circle E?"

She sighed. "I know you've been hankering after that land for a long time. I don't know how badly you want it, but I do know that if you marry Becca to get the ranch, you'll regret it one day."

Travis turned Alex in his arms, so they both danced forward. How badly *did* he want the ranch? Enough to marry a woman he didn't love?

No. Maybe if he'd never seen an ideal marriage like Hank and Alex's, he'd be satisfied with less. Besides, the reason he wanted the Circle E was so he could have time alone — at least until he found a woman who loved him like Alex loved Hank. A woman who would believe he could rearrange the mountains to suit her.

To Alex, he just said, "Nobody's said anything about marrying. Besides, I want someone like you. Someone who thinks I hung the moon. And Becca doesn't think too much of rodeo hands."

She missed a step. "Hung the moon? What are you talking about?"

"Admit it. You're so in love with Hank,

you think he hangs the stars out to shine every night."

Alex smiled wryly. "You're right, but don't tell Hank. His head is big enough already."

"Hell, he's so in love with you, he's probably climbing up into the sky right now." He watched Becca and her partner pass by them.

Alex's brow lifted. "You know, the way you look at Becca is the same way Hank looks at me."

Her words startled him so much he almost lost his smile. He didn't know he'd been looking at Becca any certain way.

Becca and her partner passed them again, and she glanced at him. His smile stretched to its limits. He saw Becca frown just before the damn saddle bronc rider twirled her away.

"I hope you're not using that smile on Becca," Alex said curtly.

Travis dragged his attention back to his sister-in-law. "What?"

"You know what I mean. The 'I'm a hotshot' smile." She poked a finger into his chest right above his heart. "The one that hides everything you're feeling right here."

His smile faded. "You mean my *mask?*"

"Mask? I never thought of it that way,

but that's exactly what it is."

His eyes narrowed. "That's what Becca called it."

Alex grinned. "She's even smarter than I thought. Hang on to this one, Travis. You need a woman who isn't going to let you get by on just a smile. One who's going to dig deep inside you to find what you're like beneath the bark."

"Bark? You calling me a dog?"

"Actually, I'm calling you a tree," she said, her face serious. "The notion occurred to me several years ago. Have you ever seen a magnolia? There's a lot of them in Alabama, where I was born."

"A magnolia? Sure. I've been to rodeos in the South."

"Then you know what they look like. They're big, beautiful trees with large, thick leaves and big waxy flowers that smell heavenly and cones kinda like a pine tree. But that's all you ever see, the leaves and flowers and cones. The branches grow so thick and so low to the ground, you can't see a magnolia's trunk."

"Yeah? So?"

"Well, I think you're like a magnolia. To the world you show only your thick shiny leaves and beautiful blooms. You look real good and smell real good. But that's all anyone knows, because that's all you let them see. The world never catches a glimpse of the thick, straight trunk holding up the whole shebang."

Once again Alex's insight surprised him. Her philosophizing was damn accurate, and it scared the hell out of him. He hadn't realized his life was all — as she put it — leaves and flowers until a few years ago.

Since his sister-in-law seemed to expect some reply, he murmured, "A magnolia, huh? I hope you're not going to call me that in public."

"There's more to my metaphor. Want to hear?"

"Might as well get it all off your chest."

"Though a magnolia's cones can end up miles away from the tree, the roots are still planted deep in the home soil. You're like that. You travel all over the continent, to this rodeo and that rodeo, but your roots are firmly planted at home. You'll settle back home one day, and I believe that when you do, you'll stay for good. Who knows? Becca may be the woman who'll help you realize where your roots are."

Struck dumb by her insight, Travis didn't know what to say. Instead, he whirled Alex a couple of times.

Was Becca the woman he'd been searching for?

When Alex settled back in his arms, she tossed him a crooked smile. "I realize this all may be coming from my own deep longing for a home and my wish to keep the family together. But what do you think?"

"You mean about the flowers or the cones?"

She shook her head in disgust. "You're as thick-headed as your brother. All I'm saying, Travis, is that you're going to have to do some heavy pruning so the right woman will be able to see the real you. Either that, or you'll have to find a woman who's willing to crawl back into the heavy branches to get to your trunk. Just make sure she doesn't get too scratched up or she'll quit before she gets there."

The song ended, and Alex pulled out of his arms. "Just think about what I said, okay? I want to see you happy."

He leaned down and fondly kissed her cheek. "I know."

She pushed at his arm. "You better be quick if you're going to claim Becca's next dance. I'm going to catch a ride to the hotel."

He easily held fast against her pressure.

"Hank'll have my hide if something happens to you. Can't you wait until after I get my buckle? We'll leave right afterward."

"Hank will have the kids in bed by now and be happy to see me." She wiggled her eyebrows at him. "Very happy."

Travis grinned. "Hank's a lucky man."

"You got that right, cowboy." Alex waved as she disappeared into the crowd.

He straightened and glanced around, spying the back of Becca's red curls bouncing as she shook her head at three cowboys. He was behind her before he even realized he'd taken a step, and quickly took advantage by circling her slender waist with his hands.

"Sorry, boys. This one's mine." He didn't know if he was talking about the woman or the dance. At the moment it didn't matter. A slow song started up. He turned Becca into his arms. She came willingly, almost gratefully, and Travis felt relief settle around his heart.

"I know your knee's hurting," he told her softly. "But since you danced a couple of times, they won't leave you alone if we try to sit one out."

She gave him a tired smile. "I'm fine."

"We'll head on back as soon as it's over."

"All right."

She leaned a little closer into him, and he pulled her the rest of the way, urging her to lay her head on his shoulder. When she did, he felt like he'd just won his first gold buckle.

As he guided them slowly around the edge of the dance floor, he considered Alex's suggestions. If he was going to find the kind of woman he wanted to share his life with, he had to reveal his true self. But how could he do that when he wouldn't recognize his true self if it rode up and raked its spurs across his face?

Alex also implied the right woman might be Becca.

Could his sister-in-law be right? Was the answer to his dreams dancing in his arms right now? Someone who would love him, who would help him discover who he was, and who owned the Circle E to boot?

No. Alex was wrong. Becca couldn't stand rodeo cowboys. Surely the right woman for the Million-Dollar Cowboy wouldn't hold his chosen profession against him.

On the other hand, she felt damn good in his arms. She fitted against him almost as if she'd been custom designed.

When the slow song ended, Travis stared down a cowboy who looked like he was about to cut in. Another song started almost immediately, a faster one, but he kept their pace at the same slow tempo.

Becca followed his movements naturally, as if one brain controlled both their bodies.

Travis breathed in the faint muskiness of her warm scent. He couldn't remember what magnolias smelled like, but her smell made the image of the beautiful white flower pop into his mind. The aroma wafted through his soul, relaxing him at the same time it tightened him with desire.

Could Alex be right? Was Becca the woman he'd been searching for all his life? What if she was? What could he do about it? He needed time alone. Time to heal.

Didn't he?

Yet somehow, time alone seemed ludicrous when he held Becca in his arms, when the memory of her kisses kept him from sleeping.

Maybe he should try Alex's suggestion. What could it hurt? If Becca was the one for him, she'd change her mind about him being a rodeo hand. If she wasn't, at least he could practice on her so he'd know what to do when the right woman did come along.

According to Alex, all he had to do was

lop off some branches.

Sounded like it was going to hurt.

"Did you talk to your momma after the go-round?" Travis asked as he pulled into the late-night traffic on Flamingo.

Becca nodded, then realized he had his eyes on the road. "For just a minute. She didn't say anything, but I'm sure she was disappointed that I didn't place first."

"You were two hundredths of a second off the lead. That's pretty damn good. You can't be first every night, you know, not when you're up against the fourteen best barrel racers in the world."

"I know. It's just that . . ."

"Just what?" he coaxed.

She sighed wearily. First place paid over two thousand dollars more than her second-place payoff, and she needed every penny she could get. "Nothing."

He reached across and laced his fingers through hers. When he settled their clasped hands on her knee, Becca's heart flipped over itself. Though there was no reason why they should be holding hands when they were alone, no one around to prove anything to, she didn't pull away. His warmth was comforting, his grip so certain, so strong.

These were the times when she found it hard to remember he was a rodeo cowboy. These were the times when she found it hard to remember her name.

He let go in order to shift, then casually — as if he had every right — retook possession of her hand.

Even in Las Vegas the traffic was light at one in the morning, so it only took a few moments to reach the Diamond Spurs. Travis found a parking space close to an entrance and eased his oversize truck in. He switched off the engine and unhooked his seat belt, but didn't make any move to get out of the truck. In fact, he once again slipped his hand around hers.

Since he'd made it plain early on that she was to wait for him to come around and open her door, she glanced at him. "What are you —"

His eyes were like blue lasers, burning away her train of thought.

"I'm going to kiss you." His husky tone rumbled deep into her soul. "I haven't been able to get our kiss the other night out of my mind. Do you think it's as good as we remember?"

His eyes kept her mesmerized as he drew closer slowly, giving her plenty of time to say no. But Becca couldn't have formed the simple word even if she'd wanted to. And God help her, she didn't want to.

His mouth finally touched hers. A tiny shock bit hard, then sped through all parts of her body.

One of them moaned — Becca didn't know who — and Travis let go of her hand to slip his arm around her waist. Now heat came from two sources. It fanned up from her hips and down from her lips, sending her heart into overdrive.

His tongue traced the outline of her lips and when she opened them, it plunged inside. Waves of pleasure threatened to suffocate her, but she didn't complain. She didn't pull away.

In fact, her arms wrapped around his neck. She knocked off his hat and drove her hands into his hair. The sensation caused a moan to well up from deep inside.

Just when she thought she might lose consciousness, they came up for air.

"Damn!" Travis uttered a bare inch away.

Becca gasped in the breath he exhaled. The heated air scorched her lungs. Her brain barely had the energy to make her lips murmur, "What?"

He thrust his hands under her bottom

and lifted her sideways onto his lap. "Never in my wildest dreams did I think it'd be *better* than I remember."

Even if she could've summoned the strength, Becca didn't have the chance to reply because his mouth took hers again, and the feeling of desertion vanished.

Heat surrounded her. Hard heat — from the hand that cradled her hip on one side, protecting it from the steering wheel, to the bulge growing against her other hip, to the lips slanting across hers.

Nothing in her life had prepared her for such an overwhelming onslaught of sensation. Never had mere lips been able to drive her will away. Never had a man's touch sent her sailing across the stars.

His hand squeezed her hip, then caressed its way up until it gently tested the weight of her breast.

Suddenly her hot blood burst into flames, burning fiery paths along every vein, incinerating her will to do anything but get closer to the source of undistilled pleasure.

She arched against his hand, making him groan and shift on the seat.

The movement drove her hip into the steering wheel. "Ow!"

Travis froze instantly, then swore into

her mouth. "I hurt you. That's the last thing I meant to do."

Disappointment sliced deep as reality intruded. "I know."

His strong, gentle hand dropped to her hip and massaged. "I'm sorry. I didn't mean to get so . . . carried away."

As he spoke he trailed soft kisses across her cheek and down her neck. In danger of succumbing to his mind-numbing heat again, Becca bracketed his face with her hands and pushed his head back. "It was my fault, too."

He turned to kiss her palm. Becca couldn't stop her thumb from rubbing across his lower lip.

"You know this changes everything."

His statement made her breath catch. "What do you mean?"

"There's no need to pretend anymore," he said. "This relationship is hereby officially declared real."

Becca felt as if ice water had suddenly infused her veins. Feeling vulnerable in Travis's arms, she struggled to climb back across the truck. "Are you out of your mind?"

He held her tight. "There's something between us. I've never felt desire this strong, and I'm ashamed to tell you how many women I've known. I aim to find out what this is."

"You just said what it is. Desire. That's all."

"Maybe. Maybe not."

She glared at him. " 'Real' was not part of our agreement."

"Things have changed."

"Speak for yourself."

His eyes narrowed, and she suddenly noticed he wasn't smiling. The fact that he'd taken off his mask for her, that he was showing her the real Travis, that the real Travis wanted her, nearly broke through her defenses. She wanted to drag his mouth back to hers and lose herself in his heat . . . forever.

"Damn it, Becca. You can't tell me you didn't feel anything." His voice lowered as one finger traced the curve of her neck. "Your heart is still racing like your mare at top speed. And you admitted you contributed as much to that kiss as I did."

No, she couldn't tell him she didn't feel anything. Then again, she couldn't tell him she did. "Will you please let me go? It's late. We need to get to bed."

He smiled a natural, sexy, genuine smile.

"Separately," she clarified.

He picked her up and placed her in the

passenger seat himself. "All right. For now. But this discussion isn't over. Not by a long shot."

Becca frowned as she searched the truck floor for her hat and jacket. That's exactly what she was afraid of.

Chapter Seven

Tuesday, Go-Round #5

Becca quietly let herself into the suite just after lunch. Hearing her mother's soft voice, she peeked around the corner into the living room and saw Joy ensconced in the chair Becca was beginning to think of as her throne.

Joy had her sewing in her lap and an enrapt audience of two small cowboys. She was telling J.J. and Matt about the time Travis drove the Larsons' small herd up to summer pastures all by himself.

Joy interrupted the story when she spied Becca. "How was practice for the fashion show, dear?"

The two young Edens spun around and chorused, "Hi, Becca."

Caught, Becca walked over and placed a kiss on her mother's cheek. "They showed me the outfits I'm going to wear. I've never changed clothes so much in my life. The last one's a bridal gown!"

Her mother's eyes twinkled. "I can't wait to see you. And it's for a good cause."

"Uncle Travis said the Justin Crisis Fund helps a lot of cowboys when they get hurt real bad," J.J. said.

Becca smiled down at the boy's serious face. "I know. I don't mind too much, even though I'll have to get up even earlier on Thursday. Where's Sarah?"

"She's taking a nap," Matt said. "She's a baby."

"Your mom and dad are meeting people at the Whitehead ranch who want to see their stock, aren't they?"

"Yes, ma'am," J.J. answered.

"Uncle Travis said you and he might take us to Circus Circus when Sarah wakes up." Matt's face was hopeful. "If you feel like it. Do you?"

She ruffled his dark hair. "I'm looking forward to it. I bet you like the clowns."

Matt shook his head. "I like the trapeze. And the lion tamers."

"They don't have lions there," J.J. told his brother, then he turned to her. "I like the clowns."

"I do, too," Joy said, drawing a smile from the older boy.

"Me, too." Becca swept off her hat and

headed toward the kids' room. "I'm going to change."

Matt giggled and pointed in the opposite direction. "Your room is that way."

"I know, silly. I thought I'd check on Sarah."

"She's in Uncle Travis's room," J.J. told her.

"She is?" Becca started back across the room. "Why?"

J.J. lifted a shoulder. "She just wanted to. When she was little she used to get up in the middle of the night and crawl in with Uncle Travis when he was home."

"Which certainly wasn't often enough to make it a habit," she murmured.

"What, dear?" Joy asked.

Becca laid her hat on the table, then paused at the door to Travis's room. "Nothing, Momma. Go on with the story. Did you tell them about the grizzly?"

"Grizzly?" Matt cried, all thought of Sarah forgotten.

"Uncle Travis fought a grizzly?" J.J. gasped.

Joy's eyes sparkled. "I was just getting to that."

The boys would be captivated for at least half an hour. Smiling, Becca opened Travis's bedroom door without hesitation, knowing he had a meeting right after lunch with members of the Professional Bull Riders organization.

He'd dropped by practice for the Pro Rodeo League of Women Fashion Show long enough to give the volunteers a thrill, and long enough to ask if Becca would help him take the kids to see some of the acts at Circus Circus. He'd kissed her soundly before he left, drawing smiles from some of the women and hostile glances from others, particularly CherylAnn.

Sarah lay facedown on the far side of Travis's king-size bed, still fast asleep. Perching on the edge of the mattress, Becca gently pushed back a strand of silky brown hair that had fallen across the child's face, then pressed a kiss on the chubby cheek.

All of the Eden kids were just like kids should be, with three distinctly different personalities. J.J. was like his father. Matt had inherited Travis's daredevil nature. But Sarah was all her own.

Becca hoped her own kids turned out as well.

The thought made her frown. She wanted children, and her mother would dearly love to know her grandchildren. However, at this point kids were too far in the future for her to even dream about. First she needed a husband, and she wasn't going to find any acceptable candidates when all she met were rodeo cowboys.

Travis's face flitted across her mind, but she pushed his image away. No matter what he said, the only thing between them was a strong sexual attraction. Which was more than she wanted there to be, and certainly all she would allow.

Becca stood abruptly and walked around the bed, hesitating at the foot. No sense disturbing the storytelling again when she could just cut through the bathrooms.

As she opened the door leading into Travis's bath she forced her mind away from the blue-eyed cowboy to the fifth go-round that night.

She had to ride her best. The way she figured it, she had to win four of the remaining six rounds in order to win the average, which would put her on top no matter how well CherylAnn did. The only other barrel racer who'd been any competition, Naomi Witherspoon, had already tipped over two barrels. The ten-second penalty put Naomi out of the —

Steam hit Becca in the face when she

opened the door to the room with the whirlpool and sauna. Gurgling filled the air. Had her mother taken a bath and forgotten to turn off the jets?

Frowning, she stepped into the room, then stopped dead as a hole appeared in the steam. Her eyes widened to their absolute limits.

Travis lounged in the whirlpool. His long arms rested on the sides of the green marble, the strong muscles clearly defined even in repose.

Hot moisture swirled around Becca, driving her temperature to dangerous heights. To compensate, her lungs dragged in more air, which just served to send her heart trampling over itself.

"Hello, monkey-face."

His voice was husky. The tones struck a chord deep inside Becca, like a heavenly harp. Unable to glance away, unable to even move, she stared into his half-closed eyes. Was it the steam, or were they bluer than usual?

"You . . . I was just . . ." She swallowed hard. "I thought you were at the PBR meeting."

He shook his head. "They were trying to talk me into running for president, so I left. I thought I'd come back and soak my leg until you finished with your fashion show."

"Oh." The comment was inane, but she couldn't help it. All she could think about was the broad, well-muscled chest visible above the rim of the tub. If she took just a few steps closer, she might be able to see all of it. All of him.

The thought made her feel as if the hot foam in the bath was fizzing in her brain.

His voice lowered an impossible octave. "You keep looking at me like that, darlin', and I'll have to insist you lock the door and join me. There's plenty of room in here for two."

His words jolted her, but not because his suggestion offended. Far from it. What shocked her was the desire to rip her clothes off and dive in after him.

Her gaze shot upward, but the change did nothing to cool her system. Since the wall behind the whirlpool was mirrored all the way to the ceiling, she had almost a bird's-eye view of the lean, strong body disguised only by the frothing water and steamy air.

Shutting her eyes tight against her need to see more, she haltingly stepped sideways across the room, staying as close to the far wall as she could. "I, um . . . didn't know you were here. I was just going through to my room to change."

"And what were you doing in my room?" he asked teasingly.

Her mind went blank. What *was* she doing in his room? "Sarah. I was checking on Sarah."

"Is she still asleep?"

Bumping into the door leading into her own bathroom, Becca blindly felt for the knob. "Yes."

"Then there's time for you to soak your knee."

"No, I —" Hearing a loud splash, her eyes flew open.

Travis stepped out of the tub without a stitch of clothing on.

Her eyes widened and her breath caught, but she didn't look away. Didn't even want to.

He walked, dripping, through the mist, like a god rising from the sea. Though his tall body was lean, bands of muscle wrapped his limbs and torso. Broad, straight shoulders narrowed down to tight hips. His thigh muscles were long and thick, defined by years of hanging on to the backs of bulls. An ugly bruise marred one of his thighs where a bull had kicked it in the third go-round.

A strong urge suddenly overcame her. She wanted to drop to her knees and place a kiss on the blue-black skin.

The idea astonished her. Where had it come from? She'd never seen a naked man before, much less touched one in such an intimate way.

Half of Becca wanted to run from the sweltering room, the other half wanted to follow the impulse. Torn between the two, she could do neither.

"Like what you see?" He stopped bare inches from her and ran a wet finger down her cheek. "I do."

"I should —" Caught in the depths of his sky blue eyes, she couldn't remember what she should be doing. She didn't want to do anything but run her hands over his wet skin, to see if he was as hot and hard as he looked.

With a muttered curse, Travis wrapped his arms around her and slanted his mouth across hers. Relieved her inaction was finally broken, she slid her arms around his waist to press closer to his length.

Water soaked through her clothes, but it merely served to conduct the sparks that flew between their bodies. His harsh breathing, his deep moans pounded like drums in her ears, driving away sanity. The wet skin under her questing hands felt like satin over steel. The hard length of his desire pulsed against her stomach.

She gasped when he tore his mouth away and lifted her. He took a step toward the whirlpool, then glanced down at her clothes and stopped. He turned toward his door, then stopped, muttering, "Sarah. The kids. Damn."

His burning blue eyes met hers through the steamy air. "I've never wanted a woman more in my life than I want you right now."

Reality knocked the breath out of her . . . or was it his words? "You can't have me," she whispered brokenly.

"I know, damn it," he growled. "Three kids and your mother are in the next room."

"Let me down."

He searched her eyes. "I don't want to."

She swallowed hard and repeated, "Let me down."

He obeyed with obvious reluctance.

She backed out of reach. "You can't have me, Travis. I'm not going to have an affair with a rodeo cowboy."

His eyes narrowed. "What if I want more than an affair?"

Her breath caught and elation flooded

through her, but she shook her head as if she could shake the pleasure away. "I've told you. I'm not going to waste my life on a rodeo cowboy."

"What, exactly, do you have against rodeo cowboys?"

"I'm not going to get into it when you're standing there buck naked." She spun around and jerked open the door to her room.

"Then we'll get into it later," he promised softly. "But make no mistake, we *will* get into it."

She closed the door quickly so he couldn't hear her groan.

The tenth barrel racer sprang from the gate into the arena and Becca guided Cocoa down the ramp, awaiting her turn in the fifth go-round. Two cowgirls controlled their anxious mounts ahead of her, the last two barrel racers of the round were behind her. Several cowboys milled around on the other side of the steel fence lining the chute. She paid them no attention as she mentally prepared herself for the ride ahead.

In her mind she traveled around the three barrels. She knew exactly where she had to start rating Cocoa at each one. She knew the points along the arena fence where she had to look in order to —

"Monkey-face!"

A strong hand squeezed her right thigh, shattering her thoughts. She glanced over in time to see Travis straighten from his perch on the fence. Already strapped into his chaps for the bull riding that followed, he smiled and gestured her closer.

She gaped at him. Didn't he know better than to disturb someone preparing to ride?

"Go away," she said bluntly. "I need to think through the turns."

"You think too much." Suddenly he caught Cocoa's right rein and pulled the horse alongside the fence. With an arm around her waist, he hauled her half out of the saddle and kissed her mouth hard.

Off balance, she grabbed his shoulders and gasped.

"That's for luck," he said huskily, then righted her in the saddle.

"What the heck do you think you're —"

"Becca Larson!"

She looked up to see the way ahead of her clear. The chute gate swung open. Huge speakers inside the arena announced her name and statistics. She glanced at Travis, who winked at her and swung down from the fence.

Hurt and disbelief flooded through her. What was Travis doing? Trying to sabotage her run? Why?

"Becca Larson! Let's go!"

Just wanting away from him, she spurred Cocoa in the flanks. She tried desperately to concentrate on her run but was sprinting back to the gate before she even had the presence of mind to rein at the first barrel.

At she passed through the gate, she heard the announcer exclaim, "Thirteen-point-nine-seven seconds for Becca Larson! The best run so far this year!"

Travis grinned as she thundered past, both thumbs pointing up.

Becca climbed from the back seat of Travis's truck and kissed her mother's cheek. "Are you sure you'll be able to get three kids into bed by yourself? I know you've had a good day today, but . . ."

Joy patted her cheek. "I'll be just fine, dear."

"I can stay if you —"

"Oh, no, you can't. You've got to get your buckle." Her mother beamed. "I'm so proud of you. I'm glad I could be there to see you win."

Hank pulled his truck up behind Travis's

at a side entrance to the Diamond Spurs. Alex helped her kids down, then walked them to where Becca and Joy waited. Alex thanked Joy profusely for taking care of the kids so she and Hank could go to the buckle presentation. After a round of hugs and kisses, the kids disappeared into the hotel with Joy.

Alex stuck her head in the open passenger door of Travis's truck. "I suggested to Hank that we ride together, but he wants to get back early."

"Fine by me," Travis told her.

Alex smiled at Becca. "We'll see you there."

Becca caught Alex's arm as she started toward the truck behind Travis's. "Is it all right if I ride with you and Hank?"

Alex turned in surprise. "Well, sure, but —"

"Oh, no, you don't!" Travis jerked his door open and came around the truck. "You're riding with me."

Becca lifted her chin. "Not if I don't want to."

He grabbed her hand. "I know you're mad. Hell, you haven't said two words to me since your ride. But I can explain."

"What explanation can you possibly have for what you did?"

"Helping you win."

Becca blinked. "What do you mean?"

Alex patted her arm. "As dearly as I would love to know what's going on, Hank's watching so I can't get in the middle of this. We'll see you at the Gold Coast."

Travis gestured to his truck. "Will you please get in? We can discuss it on the way."

Since Alex had deserted her, Becca climbed stiffly into the passenger seat of Travis's truck. He shut the door, then walked around and slipped under the steering wheel.

"What do you mean, helping me win?" she demanded.

"You beat the pants off the competition, didn't you?" he shot back.

"Well, yes. But —"

"I talked to Harriet Bradley about the trouble you've been having in the last three go-rounds. She said you have the best horse at the Finals, and that you've got good form, but that you're too uptight. You're beating yourself because you're thinking too much. I wanted to take your mind off the ride, even if I had to make you mad to do it. Even if I got in trouble to do it, and I won't repeat to a lady the words the chute boss had for me."

"Good for Buster Carlson," she murmured. But Travis had blown the wind out of her sails, and she sank back into the plush leather seat.

Travis hadn't been trying to sabotage her run. He'd gone to the trouble of finding out what she'd been doing wrong, then risked official reprimand to help her.

Was it possible she'd found a rodeo cowboy who was an exception to the rule? One who might care more for her than for rodeo?

"And I tell you one thing," he said. "I'm going to be up on that fence every night for the next five go-rounds, assuming I can get around Buster."

"But you didn't even place in the bull riding tonight. You don't need to worry about me. You need to prepare yourself for your bull ride."

"Hell, I've been riding bulls for twenty years. If I'm not prepared by now, I never will be. Besides, my seventy-three score was the bull's fault, not mine. He stood stock-still for the last three seconds of the ride. When I dropped from his back after the whistle, he sashayed through the gate like he was going to tea." They stopped at a light, and he met her eyes squarely. "I'll be there for you. Count on it."

Counting on a rodeo cowboy was something she'd thought she'd never do. Yet Becca was beginning to count on this one more and more.

Which wasn't smart. Not smart at all.

"About time you got back," Hank complained over the noise in the dance hall. "I was about to call in the National Guard to help me beat these cowboys away from your woman."

Travis set a soft drink in front of Becca, but didn't sit in the seat she'd saved for him at the small table. She glanced up. His smile was wider than she'd ever seen it, and frozen into place.

Travis leaned over the table. "Looks like I'm gonna have to ask you to continue guard duty. My biggest paying sponsor cornered me and wants me to head downtown after the presentation with him and a group of guys he brought."

Becca's heart twisted. So much for the possibility that he cared more for her than rodeo. Didn't take long for reality to set in. "So you're going to play superstar."

Travis turned to her. The look on his face confused her. If she didn't know better, she'd swear he'd rather be doing anything than schmoozing with his sponsor. His expression made her want to snatch him up, hightail it out of there and wipe the tension from his face with a thousand kisses.

But she did know better. He was, after all, a rodeo cowboy.

He touched her cheek. "Yeah, monkeyface. Will you be okay riding back to the hotel with Hank and Alex?"

She lifted a brow. "I think I can manage."

Leaning down, he kissed her cheek, whispering, "I'm sorry, darlin'. I couldn't get out of it."

She stiffened, determined not to show her disappointment. "I'll be fine. Don't worry about me."

"I'll see you in the morning. We're still on for the picnic, aren't we?"

Becca nodded woodenly. Travis straightened and said something else to Hank and Alex, but Becca barely noticed. The joy of winning had been swept away in a single phrase.

Don't worry about me.

How many times had she heard her mother say those same words to her father just before he left them for another round of rodeos? Becca had sworn she would never say those words to her own man, had sworn she wouldn't have the kind of man she'd have to say them to.

Travis disappeared back into the crowd with a final glance.

Becca straightened in her chair. Travis was not her man, and he never would be. No matter how much he helped her, she couldn't let herself go soft. She couldn't allow herself to believe he cared.

Helping people was just his nature. He'd been doing it all his life.

And she wasn't the only recipient of his assistance. He was renowned for lending his name, and smile, to charities.

That's all she was to him, another charity.

What if I want more than an affair?

His words, spoken in the steamy bath that morning, echoed through her mind. There was no mistaking his meaning — he referred to marriage.

A thrill of delight warmed her inside, even as fear sent chills skimming across her skin.

Marry Travis Eden?

He was rodeo's Million-Dollar Cowboy. Arena mud flowed in his veins. Going down the road was as natural to him as smiling.

Alex had been hinting to her that Travis

wanted out of rodeo, but Becca didn't believe her. Travis was well on track to tie history by winning his eighth bull riding championship. One more year, and he could make history by winning his ninth. Something no other cowboy had ever done.

Why would he quit rodeo now? He was at his peak. The rodeo world adored him. He made more money than any rodeo cowboy in history.

He wasn't about to throw all that away. His going off with this sponsor made that as clear as the air on Yellow Jack Mountain.

Marry Travis Eden? Not even for the deed — free and clear — to the Circle E.

Wednesday, Go-Round #6

"Matt?" Becca peered around a curve of rock in the Red Spring Picnic Area west of Las Vegas. "J.J. found a turtle. Wanna come see?"

"You bet!" Matt shouted. "Catch me, Uncle Travis!"

Travis glanced up from where Becca stood just in time to catch Matt, who'd launched himself into the air from ten feet above. Matt scrambled out of his hold and disappeared.

Becca turned to follow him.

"Wait up," Travis called.

She looked over her shoulder with obvious reluctance. "What?"

Her attitude irritated him, like it had all morning. She'd been as cool as the morning air, avoiding his eyes, his touch, his presence.

When he reached her side, he grabbed her hand, just to see what she'd do. She met his gaze, her blue eyes cool and distant, then slowly pulled her hand away.

"Damn it, Becca, what's wrong? You're acting like I'm —"

"A rodeo cowboy?" she asked primly.

Travis shoved his hat back. "You say that like we're first cousins of the devil."

She lifted one red brow.

He threw his hands in the air. "What the hell is wrong with rodeo cowboys?"

She spun to leave. "We don't need to get into this now. I need to catch up with the kids before they get too far."

He caught her arm, and before she had a chance to protest, he backed her up against the red rock wall and slanted his mouth across hers. She gasped in surprise and struggled, but within seconds she melted against him.

Relieved by her response, Travis pulled back to comment on her quick surrender.

She murmured a protest and wrapped her arms around his neck. Smiling, he let her draw him back down to her lips.

Finally, Becca broke the contact. Gasping for air, she buried her face against his neck. "Damn you."

He cupped her face with his hands, forcing her to meet his gaze. "Damn me all you like, darlin', but you can't tell me you don't want *this* rodeo cowboy."

She grimaced. "I didn't say I don't *want* you. I said I don't want you."

"Now that makes about as much sense as —"

"Becca?" Matt's call echoed around the rock, startling them both. "You coming?"

She struggled against Travis.

He let her go except for her hand. "You know this conversation isn't over, don't you?"

She rolled her eyes. "You've made that threat more than once."

"It's not a threat, darlin'. It's a promise."

She pulled her hand away. "Why don't you go check on Momma?"

He followed her escape with narrowed eyes. What the hell was so wrong with rodeo cowboys?

When she disappeared around a boulder, he turned his gaze toward the picnic area.

A column of smoke marked the place where Joy cooked hamburgers. Did Mrs. Larson know about her daughter's aversion to rodeo cowboys? And if she did, would she tell him Becca's reasons?

Only one way to find out.

Travis caught a whiff of the burgers as he entered the picnic area.

"My mouth is watering," he called.

Joy smiled from her folding chair beside the grill. "I just turned them. They'll be ready in about twenty minutes."

Not sure of the best way to approach Mrs. Larson to find out what he wanted to know, Travis pulled a cold drink from the cooler. "I wish you'd have let me pick up some fried chicken or something. It's what we usually do. I didn't mean to make you cook when I invited you."

"I know, Travis dear," she said. "But fresh food always tastes better. Besides, I like to do what I can, even though it isn't too much these days."

He sat on the end of the picnic table bench closest to her and pushed the hat back on his head. "How are you feeling?"

"I think I'll live through the day," she said wryly.

His smile faded. "How can you joke about it?"

"I have to," she said softly. "Or I'll go crazy."

He reached across the space between them and squeezed her arm. "I wish I could help."

"I wish you could, too." She sighed. "But some things are in the good Lord's hands."

"Sometimes the Lord wants us to use the resources we've got."

She patted his hand, and he removed it from her arm. "I'll be happy if I can see Becca settled before I go. I worry about her."

He took a deep swallow of the drink. "Why? According to her, she can take on the world all by herself."

Joy sprinkled water onto the grill as fat made the coals blaze. "That's what she'd like you to think, but it isn't true. She needs somebody just as badly as everyone else does. Maybe more."

Though Mrs. Larson hadn't actually asked the question, it hung in the air between them. "You sound like you're wanting to know if that somebody is me."

"I reckon I am." She looked him square in the eye. "I reckon I'm asking your intentions toward my daughter. She says you're just friends, but the way you look at each other makes me doubt it."

Travis leaned his forearms on his knees and dropped his gaze to the cold drink can in his hands. His intentions. How the hell could he have intentions when Becca acted like he was some bug crawling on her plate?

He glanced at Joy, whose eyes studied him closely. "I know this doesn't answer your question, but what's Becca got against rodeo cowboys?"

Mrs. Larson sighed and fluttered her hands. "I was afraid that might be a problem. It was her father's fault, mostly. Hoyt loved to rodeo more than he loved just about anything, I expect. Certainly more than he loved the Circle E. The ranch was doing fine when we got married. Then when my daddy died a couple years later, Hoyt took over management. Or maybe I should say mismanagement. He spent nearly every nickel we came by on entry fees. Then . . . Well, you know what happened."

They lost the ranch.

"Not all rodeo cowboys are like Hoyt."

Joy pushed herself up from the folding chair and tested the doneness of a burger. "No. It took another cowboy to drive the nails into that coffin."

"Another cowboy?" Travis's eyes narrowed. The thought of Becca with another man made the hairs rise along his spine. Somehow he hadn't even considered the possibility. What had he thought — that she'd stayed a gangling monkey-face until he found her on the side of the highway?

Becca was a beautiful woman. He knew other men desired her — enough to place a bet on who could "melt her icicles."

The idea made him want to tattoo his name across her forehead.

Realizing Mrs. Larson was speaking, Travis tuned in to the details.

". . . Bud Sager, Becca's high school sweetheart. She thought she was in love with the boy, but he up and took off to rodeo the day after he graduated. That's when Becca swore off rodeo cowboys for good." Joy idly swatted at a fly. "Bud came back a year later. Wasn't winning any money on the circuit. Becca wouldn't even bid the fella a good day."

"Then I don't stand a chance."

Travis didn't realize he'd said the words aloud until Mrs. Larson said, "She's going out with you, isn't she? She'll barely say hello to other rodeo cowboys. And I've seen the two of you kissing when you think nobody's looking.

"It's kinda interesting, the way you two

took to each other after so many years. You probably don't remember, but when Becca was little, she used to swear she'd marry you one day. You'd laugh at her and say you might even marry a monkey-face if you could live on the Circle E. I was kinda surprised you hadn't bought the ranch years before Becca contacted Sam Duggan. But I reckon what with rodeoing, you lost the hankering to settle down."

There it was again — the subtle suggestion that he marry Becca for the Circle E. This time he didn't dismiss the notion so easily.

Marrying Becca would solve all their problems. He could pay off the loan on the ranch and would have every right to pay for any medical treatment Joy needed. He'd have the Circle E, and he'd have Becca.

Did he want them both at the same time? What about his need for time alone? Time to heal?

He knew he wanted the Circle E, and he knew he wanted Becca.

But did he want her, or did he *want* her? Now Travis understood Becca's cryptic comment. Was this ache for her only lust, or something more? He wanted a marriage like Hank's, a marriage based on love with a woman who believed he could lasso the moon.

Was Becca that woman, like Alex suggested she might be?

Becca hadn't shown any tendency to believe in him so far. In fact, she'd made it perfectly clear she wouldn't consider any long-term relationship with a rodeo cowboy.

Then he remembered her kisses. Fire like that couldn't be make-believe, and they shared the hottest kisses when they were alone, when there was no need for pretense.

Travis shook his head. Hot one minute, cold the next. She was confusing the hell out of him.

"Looks like these burgers are about done," Joy said. "Why don't you go fetch Becca and the kids?"

"Yes, ma'am."

He rose stiffly, absently rubbing his left knee. He needed to get Becca alone. They had a helluva lot of talking to do. But when? She'd been avoiding him all day like he was contagious.

Then he remembered Rube Pruitt's call that morning. Becca's truck was ready. They'd already talked about getting up early the next morning and driving to Glendale.

Travis grinned. He'd have at least an hour alone with her on the way. A captive audience.

Chapter Eight

Thursday, Go-Round #7

Travis glanced over at Becca. She watched the outskirts of Las Vegas passing by as they headed northeast toward Glendale to retrieve her truck. "You're quiet this morning."

She shrugged. "What do you expect when you don't let me get to bed until two and then made me get up at eight?"

"You're the one who has to be back at ten so you can prance around on a stage in fancy outfits."

"I know." Becca shot him a narrow-eyed gaze. "But when I agreed to model in the fashion show I didn't know I'd be so busy this week. I figured it was the only thing I'd be doing besides riding every night."

"You blaming me?" His hand captured hers and settled on his thigh. He was gratified when she didn't try to pull away.

She did, however, sigh heavily. "Yes and

no. It's not your fault my truck broke down. But on the other hand, your little scheme takes up all my time. Is it even working? Is CherylAnn leaving you alone?"

"Haven't heard a peep out of her since we started billing and cooing."

"Well, if it's working, I guess it's worth it." The words were spoken with definite reluctance.

"Getting to know me again hasn't been worth it?" He smiled in spite of the frown she tossed his way.

She ignored his question. "CherylAnn's certainly been throwing nasty looks at me. And last night when I rode right before her, she kept crowding Cocoa with her gelding."

"Petty revenge sounds like her." His smile faded. "Sorry I couldn't make it to the fence last night. Buster wouldn't let me through."

Becca smiled wryly. "Worrying about you showing up at any minute produced the same results."

She'd placed first again last night in the sixth go-round.

They rode quietly for a few minutes. Having had a day to dwell on the subject without even a minute alone with Becca to kiss her, Travis had boiled down what he needed to know.

Did Becca care for him at all? Could she want him as much as she *wanted* him?

Now he wondered how to go about finding out. Finally he decided to get her own version of why she hated rodeo cowboys.

When the city was finally behind them, Travis cleared his throat. "Time for our little chat."

She threw him a sharp glance. "What chat?"

"About why you hate rodeo cowboys."

Becca drew her hand from his and turned to stare out the truck window. "I don't hate rodeo cowboys."

"You said you wouldn't marry one."

"I won't."

"Why?"

"That's none of your business."

Travis set the cruise control. Sounded like Becca had already had their little chat in her mind and had decided it was in her best interest not to tell him anything. Tough. "What concerns my woman concerns me."

"I'm not your woman. Our relationship is make-believe."

"The hell it is. Make-believe went out the window the first time we kissed."

She crossed her arms over her stomach. "How can I be your woman when that implies . . . things I would never do with a rodeo cowboy?"

"Like making love?"

"Exactly."

"Darlin', there've been a couple of times when, if we'd been anywhere near a bedroom and alone, we'd have already made love — with your full consent and cooperation."

Crimson flooded her cheeks, and she turned away with a huff. "If I'd known this was going to be an inquisition, I'd have caught a bus."

Time to take another tack. "So catch me up on the past fifteen years. Where did you and your mother go after you left Wyoming?"

She regarded him suspiciously, then evidently decided the question was harmless. "Paris, Texas. Momma had a cousin who worked on a ranch there. She cooked until she got too sick. Jack — he was Momma's cousin — taught me to train horses. He died about eight years ago, and the foreman kept me on in Jack's job."

"Is that where you came by Cocoa?"

Becca nodded with a fond smile. "Cocoa's mother died when she was born.

Uncle Jack didn't think she'd live, but I begged and begged him to let me try to bottle-feed her. It was touch-and-go for a while, but eventually she became as strong as all the other horses. Since Cocoa thought I was her mother anyway, Uncle Jack gave her to me."

"It's hard to believe a horse that good just started rodeoing a year ago."

"That's not exactly true. I went to jackpot rodeos in Texas and Oklahoma to earn extra money. The foreman didn't mind because it was advertising for the ranch, let people know I was there to train their horses."

Travis nodded. Her story explained a lot. He let a full minute slide by before he steered the conversation back to where he wanted it. "Is it all cowboys, or just rodeo cowboys?"

She rolled her eyes and stared at the road so long he thought she wasn't going to answer. Finally she said, "Just rodeo cowboys."

When she didn't elaborate, he pressed. "Do we smell bad? Not make enough money? Wear our jeans too tight?"

"Of course not."

"Then what?"

"Anyone ever tell you you're as stubborn

as the bulls you ride?"

"Yep. Then what?"

She rested clenched fists on her knees. "You're never home. I want a man who'll be there when I need him. A man who doesn't lose all our money on entry fees. A man who'll be with me when our children are born, who'll be there to help raise them. A man who loves me more than he loves rodeo. Is that too much to ask?"

Surprised by her passionate response, he answered quietly, "No, that's not too much to ask."

"Now do you understand why you don't fit the description?"

"I'm not like your dad, Becca."

Her chin tilted up. "How are you different?"

Time for this magnolia tree to hack off a few branches, like Alex suggested. Instead of being reluctant, however, Travis discovered he wanted to let Becca know who he was. Maybe he'd learn something about himself in the process. "We're different in lots of ways. The most obvious, of course, is that I don't often lose my entry fee. Between my rodeo winnings and my sponsorships, I make a damn good living. Most of which I hand over to Claire, who invests it for me. I've got more money than a penny-pincher like you would spend in a lifetime."

Though saving wasn't typical of any cowboy — they usually spent money before it burned a hole in their jeans — Becca believed him. Travis had earned more than a million dollars just from rodeo winnings, plus whatever his sponsors paid him. And from what she'd seen, he didn't blow money like a lot of cowboys, buying rounds of drinks for the house and a new truck every year. Travis's rig was top of the line, but it was several years old.

Money, however, was the least important attribute of her ideal man. "I don't care how much money you have. You're like my father in the most important way. You're never home."

"Only because I don't have a home."

"What? Of course you have a home." She slapped her forehead. "Oh, silly me. You're never there so you probably forgot. It's called the Garden. Remember now?"

"The Garden is Hank's home, not mine. He and Alex have filled the house at the Garden with love and children. I feel out of place whenever I stay there." He gave her an unreadable look. "I've been trying to buy some land nearby but haven't had any luck so far."

Becca studied his profile as he drove. "Are you saying you'll quit rodeo when you buy your own ranch?"

"In a heartbeat."

"I don't believe you."

Frustration clouded his face as he threw her a swift glance. "Why the hell not? I'm sick of rodeoing. Driving long, hard hours just to land in the dirt. I want peace and quiet for a change. I want to stay in one place. As Alex put it, I want to find my roots."

Becca's brows tried to meet. Her father had never talked like this. He'd never gotten sick of the road. Still . . . "You're rodeo's Million-Dollar Cowboy. How can you quit?"

"Easy. All I have to do is stop paying entry fees."

"You'll lose your sponsor money."

He shrugged. "In a year or two."

"You're about to make history by winning your eighth bull riding championship. One more year and you could break Don Gay's record."

"There's no guarantee I'll win anything. I could break my leg tonight."

"But what if you win this one, won't you be tempted to go for the ninth?"

"No."

Her clenched fists pounded her thighs. "Why are you doing this? You sound like you're trying to talk me into marrying you, and we both know that would never work."

He captured her hand and asked softly, "Why not, monkey-face? Don't you like me at all?"

Becca stared down at their joined hands. Like him? Yes, she liked him. Way too much for her own comfort. She might even be well on her way to loving him, but she refused to think about that. If she refused to entertain the possibility, maybe she could prevent it from happening. "Are you asking me to marry you?"

His brow creased as he drove along. After a few minutes he answered, "No. I just want you to loosen up with me like you've done with your riding. Maybe we can win at this, too."

"Are you . . ." She cleared the lump from her throat. "Are you in love with me?"

His frown deepened. "I don't know. I do know I want you more than I've wanted any woman in a long, long time."

She shook her head. "We've already discussed that. It's just lust. It'll go away when I do."

"Maybe. And maybe it won't. Maybe the

thought of you going away makes me want to slip my bridle on you and tie you to the nearest fence."

"Try it, and I'll kick you from here to kingdom come."

Suddenly his frown broke into a chuckle. He wiggled his eyebrows and squeezed her hand. "Sounds like fun."

"I'm serious, Travis."

"Me, too, monkey-face. Now answer my question."

"What question?"

"Do you like me at all?"

She tried to drag her hand from his, but he held fast. "You know I do."

"No, I don't. Why do you think I have to ask? One minute you're snuggling up to me, the next you're spitting in my face."

"That's because . . ." She trailed away, uncertain of how much she wanted to reveal.

"Because what?" He shifted so their fingers were intertwined. "I opened up for you. Can't you do the same?"

In a quiet, uncertain voice, she told him, "Because I'm afraid."

His glance was incredulous. "Of me?"

"Of the way you make me feel. I've never felt this way with any other man, especially not a rodeo cowboy."

His voice lowered. "How do I make you feel?"

Trust him to ask. How could she possibly put these feelings into words? "Confused. Tingly inside. Out of breath. Wanting to be with you. Wanting to touch you. Wanting to forget you're a rodeo cowboy."

"Then forget I ever paid an entry fee," he said softly. "I'm a man, darlin'. A man who's just as confused and tingly inside and out of breath. A man who wants to be with you and touch you in places no man has ever touched you before. Can you pretend I'm just a man so we can discover what's real between us and what isn't?"

His words poured over her like warm honey, and she took a deep, ragged breath to cool herself off. He was asking too much. They were at the National Finals, for goodness' sake. How could she forget he was a rodeo cowboy when rodeo surrounded them every waking minute?

And what if she fell in love with him? No matter what he said, he was a rodeo cowboy, and she'd sworn for the past fifteen years that she would never have anything to do with rodeo cowboys. How could she dismiss so easily the premise she'd lived by for so long?

"Would it be so hard?" he asked when

she didn't reply. "You've been pretending to like me for five days and have everyone convinced. Can't you convince me, too?"

The pretending wasn't what she had a problem with. Actually, there would be no pretense. All she had to do was let down her guard. She already liked him. She liked the way his fake smile turned genuine when their eyes met. She liked the patience he showed with his niece and nephews. She liked the way he took care of things, the way her mother relaxed around him. What worried her was what letting down her guard might lead to. "I don't know . . ."

"You already said you like me. All I'm asking you to do is determine how much." His thumb rubbed the back of her hand. "Can you do that for me? Please?"

Do it for him. How could she refuse? He'd done so much for her, and for her mother. Maybe that's all these feelings for him were — just gratitude. Maybe if she went along with his suggestion, she'd discover she only liked him as a friend, like when she was a child. "All you want is for us to date. For real, I mean."

"Right. No lifetime commitments. No pressure. Just dating."

"And you've probably dated hundreds of girls without a commitment."

"Well, I wouldn't say hundreds . . ."

"So odds are, I'll just be another one."

He squinted at her. "Every now and then, somebody beats the odds."

She dismissed his comment with a wave of her hand. "I've never been lucky." And in this case, she wanted to be unlucky. "Okay. I'll do it. Although . . . What exactly is going to change? You've been treating me pretty much the same when we're alone as you do in public."

"Oh, I wouldn't say that. I don't kiss women in public the way I kissed you in the whirlpool room the other day." He gave her a sexy smile. "As a matter of fact, why don't you slide on over here and let's seal this bargain with a kiss?"

"When you're driving down the highway at seventy miles an hour? I don't think — What are you doing?"

"I'm pulling over."

"But —"

"Darlin', I aim to get my kiss one way or another."

Becca stood behind the curtain, waiting for her last trip down the runway. She was the final model, arrayed in a bridal gown that was old-fashioned, yet modern — a cross between something her grandmother might've worn and more modern creations of lace and froth. As she arranged the folds of the skirt, she heard a tittering among the ladies working behind the scenes. Glancing back through the veil attached to a pure white Stetson to see what caused the flutter, she froze.

Travis walked straight toward her, a grin spread across his face, his eyes raking down her dress. Instead of his usual casual attire, he wore a tuxedo that looked like it had been cut around him.

"Finally!" Mrs. McCowen waved him toward the stage steps. "I was beginning to wonder if he was going to show up."

Becca groaned. "You're expecting him?"

The fashion show supervisor patted Becca's arm. "He's our little surprise. I arranged it with him Tuesday. He's going to escort you down the runway."

"Why?"

"Every bride needs a bridegroom. Oh, the audience is going to get such a thrill!" With that, she stuck her head between the curtains to say something to the announcer.

"But —"

Suddenly Travis was at her side, smiling

down at her. "You look beautiful, monkey-face."

If she thought she could make it without him catching her, she'd turn right around and run down the steps. "What are you doing here?"

"Mrs. McCowen cornered me Tuesday when I stopped by to see you. Seemed to think I'd give the ladies in the audience something to talk about."

"I'll say you will. Don't you know what people are going to think when they see us together dressed like this?"

He shrugged. "Who cares?"

"I do! You can't just —"

"You ready?" Mrs. McCowen turned back to them and gave them both a critical last-minute glance.

"No," Becca exclaimed.

"What's the matter?" the supervisor asked with a worried frown. "Is there a pin bothering you?"

"She's fine." Travis pulled Becca's hand through his arm. "We're ready."

Mrs. McCowen fluffed the veil once again as the announcer started the spiel about the designer of her gown. Then the curtain parted.

"Smile!" Mrs. McCowen hissed.

Becca automatically pasted a smile on

her face as Travis stepped forward into the bright lights.

A gasp went up from the audience, and twice as many cameras flashed as during her previous trips down the runway. She knew at least one of those was Alex's, who sat on the first row of tables with Becca's mother and Travis's sister, Claire, who'd flown into Las Vegas with her husband that morning. What they were going to think about this, Becca tried hard not to imagine.

Travis guided them to the beginning of the runway, then stopped. When she felt him turn his head toward her, she looked up.

He smiled down at her — the perfect groom.

She was going to kill him. Through the gritted teeth of her smile, she said, "I'm going to get you for this."

His smile widened, and there was a definite twinkle in his blue eyes. "Promise?"

Uncomfortable from the heat in his gaze, Becca tore her eyes from his. "Let's get this over with."

He obediently stepped down the runway. He escorted her slowly, as befitting a bride, milking the sensation they were causing for all it was worth. Becca wanted to scream.

When they were halfway, where Alex and Claire sat to the left, Becca glanced down to see Alex adding to the deafening applause and Claire grinning up at her brother with two thumbs up. Joy had tears in her eyes.

Becca was going to kill the whole Eden clan. She spent the rest of their slow trip down the runway and back fantasizing about how she was going to perpetrate the mass murders.

When they finally reached the beginning of the runway again, Travis paused and turned them back around to face the audience. He pulled his arm away, then turned her toward him and lifted the veil.

Becca's eyes widened. "Don't you dare!"

His arm caught her waist as he bent his head. "Every trip down the aisle ends in a kiss."

"If you do, I'll never —"

His lips cut off her words, and suddenly the audience vanished.

Travis turned his truck into the late-afternoon traffic on Tropicana Avenue and headed toward the Thomas and Mack Arena. "All right, I can't stand this silent treatment. Let me have it."

"Let you have what?" Becca asked tonelessly.

He glanced at her. He hadn't seen her since the fashion show earlier that afternoon. Afterward, Claire had shooed him off, then she and Alex had whisked Becca away. Becca had been looking clear through him ever since she got back, which had him wondering what his sisters had said to her. "You know what. You're mad at me for walking you down the aisle."

"It wasn't an aisle. It was just a runway," she pointed out. "It's not important."

"It was important enough to make you spittin' mad three hours ago."

She shrugged. "That was three hours ago."

"So what happened since then?"

She finally looked at him. "You sound like you want me to be mad."

"I want you to be something. Ever since you came back from your afternoon with Claire, you've been acting like I'm not here. What did she say to you?"

She turned her gaze back out the window. "Nothing."

"Like hell." Travis hit the turn signal and guided the truck into one of the left-turn lanes at Swenson Street. "Damn it, Becca, talk to me."

"What do you want me to say?"

"I want you to tell me why you're acting this way."

"What way?"

"You can yell at me if you want to. You can even throw things if you have to. But you can't act like I don't exist. I won't let you."

"No, I guess you won't let me ignore you. The Million-Dollar Cowboy can't stand to be out of the limelight." She frowned. "And you expect me to believe you want to quit rodeo, to settle down."

"I do."

"I don't believe you."

"Damn it! What can I do to convince you?"

She regarded him solemnly. "I don't know that you can."

"Just this morning you said you would loosen up for me, so we can tell if there's anything real between us."

"I said I'd try."

He pulled into a parking space and switched off the engine. "You're not trying at all. You're doing everything you can to keep your heart away from me."

She gasped softly. "Is that what you want? My heart? Are you absolutely sure?"

Travis hesitated. Was her heart what he

wanted? Or was it her land? Or her body? "I'm not sure of anything. That's why we decided to get to know each other, wasn't it?" When she didn't answer, he pushed. "Well, wasn't it?"

She squeezed her eyes closed. "I guess so."

Relieved by her concession, he placed a hand over the ones she had clenched in her lap and asked quietly, "Then what's changed since then?"

"Nothing. I don't know. I just . . ."

"What did Claire and Alex say to you? Or do to you?"

Finally she looked at him, her eyes bleak. "They treated me like I was part of your family."

His brows came together. "You don't like my family?"

"No, I do," she cried softly. "I want . . . I like . . . I've never been part of a family like yours. The closest I've ever come is when I was little and you came over all the time. But your family then wasn't like it is now. Big. Boisterous. Close. I've always wanted a large family, but there's only been Momma and me."

"Then what's the problem?"

Tears made her eyes as clear as crystals. "I don't know whether I'm falling in love with you or your family."

Travis felt as if he'd been shot to the moon. *Falling in love with you.* Though coupled with doubt, her words offered hope. Reaching under the seat, he pushed back from the steering wheel, then lifted Becca onto his lap. She came without protest, and he rewarded her with a kiss.

She groaned into his mouth, then pulled away and buried her face in his neck. "Don't. You just confuse me more."

He took off her hat and smoothed the curls back from her face. "Sweet little monkey-face. My family is part of me and will be a big part of our lives if we're together. It's okay to love them, as long as you love me, too."

"But how do I know if I do?"

"Hell, I don't know. When I visited Claire and Jake at Thanksgiving, I asked her how she knew she was in love with him. She said that suddenly you just know. I guess it sorta sneaks up on you."

"Did she say how long it takes?"

He shook his head. "I imagine it's different for everybody."

Becca sighed heavily. "That doesn't help much, does it?"

"Nope. I don't reckon it does." He drew a finger across the silk of her cheek. "You like me, don't you?"

After a moment's hesitation, she admitted, "Yes."

"And you want me."

Color stained her cheeks, but she nodded bravely.

"I like you, too. A helluva lot. And I want you so bad most times I'm around you I'm ready to bust." His thumb stroked her bottom lip, and her tongue came out to lick it. He groaned. "Like now. If you said the word, I'd take you to the nearest motel and keep you naked for a week."

She caught a sharp breath. "What about the last four go-rounds of the Finals?"

He'd almost forgotten. She had to earn the money to pay off the loan on the Circle E. "Right. The National Finals Rodeo. That's why we're here, isn't it?"

She looked down, but not before he saw her face change subtly, as if she were disappointed. "Yes."

With a finger under her chin, he lifted her face back to his. "Have I finally convinced you to give me a chance?"

She swallowed hard. "You're still a rodeo cowboy."

"Becca," he said threateningly.

"Okay. All right. I will."

He smiled with relief. They were certainly a pair. She didn't know whether she was in love with him or his family. He didn't know if he was in love with her or her ranch.

He lowered his mouth to hers. The kiss they shared was poignant and sweet. A promise.

Of what, he wasn't sure. But for now, it was enough.

Chapter Nine

Friday, Go-Round #8

"Becca?"

She woke with a start. The room was dark, but she could see a large figure bent over her. She knew his smell instantly. Travis. Alarm made her rise to her elbows. "What is it?"

"Get dressed and come with me, okay?" he whispered. "I want to show you something."

Becca pushed a heavy curl from her face. "What time is it?"

"Five-thirty."

"What?"

"Shh." He sat on the side of the bed. "Don't wake your mother."

"Travis, what are you doing in here at five in the morning?"

"We're going to be with the family all day. I just want some time alone with you." His hands found hers in the darkness. "Please?"

She sighed. "Well, I'm awake now. Where are we going?"

"To a very special place for breakfast." She could hear his smile in his words. "Dress warm. I'll wait for you in the living room."

An hour later they were driving up a steep, rocky road between two red rock mountains. Travis had stopped at a fast-food restaurant for biscuit sandwiches and a thermos of coffee. Having finished a cup as they drove across the desert, Becca was wide awake when he pulled to a stop on top of a mountain.

"Here we are. Like the view?"

Becca looked out over the valley. The lights of Las Vegas twinkled in the distance, but couldn't rival the bright pink dawn. "It's beautiful."

He smiled. "I thought you'd like it. Grab the grub, okay?"

He reached into the back seat for a pile of blankets, then came around to open her door. They settled on the thick cushion of blankets he spread out, then devoured their breakfast as the sun burst above the mountains in the east.

When the show was at its most beautiful, Becca turned to Travis. "Thanks for bringing me. It's worth missing sleep. How did you find this place?"

"Some old rodeo hand told me about it years ago. I make it a point to come here at least once during Finals. Kinda puts everything in perspective."

Becca wrapped her hands around the warm coffee cup and couldn't help asking, "Do you come alone?"

He shrugged. "Usually. I brought Cheryl-Ann once, when we were together. She wasn't impressed."

She smiled wryly. "I can imagine."

"It was my first clue that she and I didn't have a helluva lot in common."

"To tell the truth, I wouldn't have figured you for the 'get up early to watch the sunrise' kind of guy myself."

"No?" He quirked one brow. "What kind of guy did you have me figured for?"

She gestured toward the city. "Like Las Vegas. All bright lights and glitter, with no real substance."

"And now?"

She shrugged and looked away from his piercing blue eyes. "Now I don't know what to think about you."

"Yes, you do, monkey-face," he said softly. "You just don't want to admit that you might be wrong about rodeo cowboys."

Her chin lifted slightly. "I have more

proof that *I'm* right, than that you are."

He scooted closer and pulled her face around to his. "You saw through my mask when no one else could. What do you think it covered?"

The tender look on his face made her want to lean into him, to kiss him and hold him and love him until they melted into the rock. But his words intrigued her. "What?"

"I smile so no one will know how sick I am of the life I lead. How tired I am of the road. How empty my days are." He bent toward her and added, "Or were."

His kiss was gentle. The heat created was like the slow burning embers of a fire, rather than the flames she'd come to expect.

When he pulled back, he searched her eyes.

She knew he couldn't help but see her worry. "Travis, I don't —"

"Let's enjoy the sunrise, okay?" He arranged them so they both faced east, with Becca between his legs.

When he put his arms around her, she leaned against his broad, warm chest with a sigh. They watched the sun rise in silent splendor for a few moments before Becca asked quietly, "Why haven't you quit if you're burned out?"

"I've tried. For the past two or three years, I go back to the Garden after the Finals, swearing I'm through. Then I can't stand being there. To tell the truth, I'm flat-out jealous of Hank. He has so much love from Alex and the kids. I guess I feel left out."

"They love you."

"I know." He lifted one hand helplessly. "It's just not the same."

"What about the land you want to buy?" she asked.

"It's not for sale."

"Where is —"

"What about you?" he asked quickly. "You told Hank you might quit barrel racing this year. Is that because of your mother?"

She wondered at his abrupt change of subject, but decided to let it go. He'd obviously opened all he was going to open right now. She'd learned more about him than she'd ever expected. "Yes. I can't leave Momma alone to go off barrel racing. Anything could happen."

He squeezed her gently. "So you're going to train barrel racers for us? Hank's been talking about finding someone for several years now."

Becca nodded. "I'm glad he needs someone. I was wondering how we were going to eat while I got my barrel racing school going."

"A school's a good idea, too. Now that you're a finalist, you've got the credentials to draw students." He settled his chin on her shoulder. "I was thinking about organizing my own bull riding clinic. You know, several weeks a year. Hank built that indoor arena several years back so we already have the chutes in place. It's a perfect setup."

They talked quietly about their plans for the future for another hour, until the sun was well above the horizon. At times it almost seemed as if they were planning their future together.

Thank goodness Becca knew better.

Becca reached across the pile of crayons on the coffee table and smoothed back a strand of Sarah's hair. "I think someone's ready for a nap."

The three-year-old quickly tried to stifle her yawn. "No, I wanna stay with you and finish my picture."

Becca patted the girl's head. "I'll be here when you wake up. And so will the coloring book."

Travis leaned over from where he'd been sitting on a couch directly behind Becca, talking with his family while Becca colored with Sarah. For the past hour, his knees had bracketed her shoulders, and his boots had cradled her hips, encasing her with warmth.

"You don't want to sleep through Becca's ride tonight, do you?" he asked his niece. "You know how Cocoa runs faster when she hears you yelling."

Sarah scrunched up her face. "Okay."

Across from them Alex started to rise, but Travis waved her back down. He lifted one leg over Becca's head, then stood and scooped up his niece. "C'mon, cricket. I'll tell you a story."

"Will you tell me the story about the princess and the bull rider?" Sarah asked with another yawn.

"You got it."

When Travis started for the kids' room, Sarah said, "No. I wanna sleep in your room."

"Fine by me," Travis told her. "But we'd better ask your momma."

Alex rolled her eyes. "I guess it's all right since J.J. and Matt are watching TV in her room, but don't go thinking you can sneak in there in the middle of the night again, young lady. You're not a baby anymore."

"I know, Momma." Sarah smiled sleepily at her mother, then laid her head on Travis's shoulder.

Becca watched them disappear into his room, then turned to find Alex smiling at her. Becca returned the smile self-consciously, then shifted her gaze to find Claire regarding her with the same knowing expression. It was enough to make a person scream.

They'd all been taken to lunch at a fancy restaurant by Claire's new husband, Jake Anderson, who seemed to have more money than most banks. Becca tried to beg out of the family occasion, but Claire had insisted she and her mother go. Afterward, everyone returned to Travis's suite to visit.

Not wanting to intrude on the Edens' family time anymore, Becca tried to sneak out of the room with her mother when Joy escaped to lie down, but Sarah quickly found her and dragged her out to color. The way Travis had smiled at his niece, Becca suspected he'd sent the girl after her.

Since she didn't want to point out Travis's devious nature in front of his family, however, she'd sat on the floor at his feet, trying to avoid being drawn into the loving circle of this close-knit family. She knew it would hurt to be excluded when she and Travis didn't marry like everyone seemed to expect, so she didn't want to get used to the warm, fuzzy feeling.

So far she hadn't been very successful. The Edens included her in their conversation as naturally and easily as Sarah shared her crayons. Everyone in the room made it clear they were happily accepting her as part of the Eden clan.

Though she kept trying to tell Alex and Claire that nothing was settled between her and Travis — especially not marriage — the pair refused to listen.

Needing something to occupy her mind and hands, Becca reached for the crayons, meticulously replacing them in their well-worn box, grouping them by color.

Was she in love with Travis? Becca thought she knew what she wanted — or rather, didn't want — when it came to rodeo cowboys. But ever since Travis stopped alongside the highway she felt as if she'd been swept along by a flash flood. A flash flood named Travis Eden.

What was wrong with her? Two weeks ago, she never would've let herself be swept away by any man, much less a rodeo cowboy. Now she was all but helpless against Travis's determination to make her part of his life.

When the crayons were neatly stacked on top of the coloring book, Becca pulled her knees to her chest, leaned back against the couch and tried to listen to Hank and Jake's discussion about the temperament of black Angus bulls.

Travis came back into the room a few minutes later.

"She didn't even last until the princess got to the arena," he told Becca and Alex. He maneuvered onto the couch, placing Becca once again between his legs. He casually worked his hands under her hair to rest on her shoulders. As he joined in the conversation with a wry comment about a black Angus bull he'd ridden that year, his thumbs rubbed lazy circles on the back of her neck.

Becca settled deeper against him with a sigh. She couldn't deny she craved his touch. When they were connected like this, she felt as if the bond would last forever. At least, she wanted it to.

Did that mean she was in love? She was beginning to suspect she might be.

There were other clues. The giddy feeling she got when she saw him for the first time each day. How she unconsciously searched for his tall figure in every crowd, listened for his deep, rumbling voice. The shivers that danced across her skin when he smiled at her. The fire that spread through her body when he kissed her. And she craved his kisses more than she craved food.

He was her first thought when she woke in the morning and her last thought at night. He even crept into her dreams.

Travis Eden was the stuff her physical fantasies were made of. He fulfilled her emotional fantasies, as well, by going out of his way to help her and her mother. In just one short week, she'd come to depend on him. That dependence scared her so much sometimes she wanted to pack her mother and Cocoa up and bolt from Las Vegas.

Other times she wanted to lean on his strength, like she was doing now.

If only she could be certain he loved her more than he loved rodeo. How could she be sure? How could he prove it?

He almost did, yesterday afternoon when he said he wanted to take her to the nearest motel and keep her there for a week. But he didn't really mean it. When he thought about it, the Finals meant more to him than she did.

Would she have gone with him if he'd been willing to give up his eighth bull riding championship for her? Would she have given up her own chance to win the barrel racing championship, and the money to pay off the loan on the Circle E?

In a heartbeat.

Heat flushed the surface of her skin as she thought of lying naked in his arms, his warmth wrapped around her. The prospect drove everything else from her mind. Even the needs of her mother, who was all she had left in the world.

A shudder — half desire, half shame — quivered down her spine.

"Are you cold?" he asked close to her ear.

She shook her head and murmured, "I'm fine."

Fine? She might — at that very moment — be falling in love with a rodeo cowboy. The worst possible thing she could do.

Would she ever be fine again?

After making sure Sarah and Matt were safely buckled in, Travis closed the back door on Hank's crew cab truck.

He placed a hand on the small of Becca's back as he walked her around the front.

"Maybe I should go with you."

"Why?" she asked with obvious impatience. "So you can protect us from the big bad wolf?"

"It's late," he argued. "And this town is —"

"Perfectly safe, from what I've seen." She reached for the handle of the driver's door and pulled it open. "At least around the hotel. The parking lot is well lit and people are coming and going all the time."

"I'll protect her," Matt exclaimed from the back seat.

"Me, too!" Sarah chimed in.

Becca climbed up under the steering wheel, and Travis moved inside the open door. "I'd feel better if I saw you to the suite."

She slipped the key into the ignition. "You can't. You've got to meet your sponsor at the —"

"To hell with the damn sponsor," he growled. "You're more important."

Becca turned to him suddenly, as if surprised. After searching his face, she lifted a hand and ran it along the stubble on his jaw. "Do you mean that?"

"I wouldn't say it if I didn't mean it."

She leaned over and kissed him. It was the first time she'd initiated physical contact. Every muscle in his body went hard with the need to drag her out of the truck so he could feel the length of her body against his. Finally she was turning to him. Finally she realized she needed him.

When she would've pulled away after brief contact, he held her shoulders and prolonged the kiss, ignoring the smacking sounds Matt made in the back seat.

Travis didn't like Becca going off without him. Not one damn bit. He'd gotten used to her being with him every night at the buckle presentation, dancing with her, having her all to himself on the drive back to the hotel, kissing her senseless before they finally walked arm in arm up to the room. The only reason he let her go at that point was he knew he had to, at least until they made up their minds whether or not this was really love and got hitched.

At the moment he was ready to find the nearest preacher, just so he'd never have to feel the wrench of parting again.

When he finally released her, she pushed herself up with a hand on his shoulder. With another lingering caress of his face, she said softly, "You go get your buckle. We'll be fine."

"But —"

She placed a finger across his lips. "I

need to check on Momma, anyway. I'm worried that she left so early. Alex said she was just tired, but I want to make sure."

"If I'd known your mother had already gone back to the hotel, I'd never have encouraged Hank and Alex to go to supper with Jake and Claire. I thought your mother would go back with the kids so you could go with me. I told my sponsor I'd be bringing you."

"I'm sure no one will miss me. You'd better go on now, or you'll miss your ride. Say good night to your uncle, kids."

As his niece and nephews chorused the sentiment, Travis growled in frustration. He dragged Becca's head down for another kiss, then forced himself to let go of her. Closing the door, he knocked on the window and pulled out his wallet. When the window was down, he handed her a ten-dollar bill. "Use the valet parking."

She shook her head. "That's too —"

"This is no time for your penny-pinching. I want you safe. If I don't find a parking stub on my dresser when I get in, I'll . . ." He let the sentence drift off, remembering there were kids in the car.

Her chin lifted in challenge. "You'll do what?"

"Will you spank her?" Sarah asked innocently.

Travis smiled wickedly as the image of his hand on Becca's bottom flashed across his mind. But his hand sure as hell wouldn't be inflicting pain. "Now there's a thought."

Becca's eyes narrowed. "Try it, buster, and you'll draw back a stub."

"J.J., you make sure Becca heads for the valet, okay?"

"Yes, sir," the older boy answered from the front seat.

Becca started the engine, then strapped herself in.

"I'll see you in the morning," Travis said as she put the truck in gear.

She gave him a cool look. "If you're lucky."

"Always have been," he told her, his grin widening.

As he watched them roll away, his smile faded. He felt as if a part of himself was driving away in that truck — and she was only taking the kids to the hotel a few miles away.

How was he going to feel if she drove out of his life when the Finals were over?

Suddenly he knew he wasn't going to let her go. He couldn't. Somehow he knew that if he did, he'd never see her again. How would he be able to stand a life without Becca when just knowing he wouldn't see her again until morning made him want to bash in the nearest wall?

This had to be love. What else could make him so happy and so miserable, so frustrated and so content?

Hell, he didn't know, and he'd never be able to convince Becca if he couldn't convince himself. She wouldn't settle for less than love. Neither would he.

There were only two days left in the Finals. He'd better make up his mind pretty damn quick.

Becca shifted under the covers and glanced at the clock again. Twelve-fifteen. She was bone tired. She needed to sleep, but Travis kept invading her thoughts.

What was she going to do about this rodeo cowboy? Should she listen to her heart and marry him if he asked, hoping he was telling the truth about quitting rodeo? Or should she listen to her head?

Questions that had no answers. Wanting to escape from them, Becca finally decided to check on the kids. Since her bedroom was close to the main door to the suite, she knew neither Travis nor

Hank and Alex had returned.

She glanced at her mother as she sat up. When Becca came in, she hadn't seen any evidence that Joy had taken medicine, so she knew her mother had just been tired like Alex said. Thank goodness.

Slipping on a pair of jeans under her T-shirt, Becca quietly left the bedroom. She padded across the suite and opened the door to the kids' room. Matt slept on one bed, still tucked in neatly. J.J. had already torn the covers completely off the other bed. The boys were just the opposite at night to what they were during the day, which made Becca smile. She'd learned a lot about children during her time taking care of the Eden kids. She couldn't wait to have kids of her own.

An insidious voice deep in her mind told her she could have a baby within a year if she married Travis. There were so many reasons why she should marry him, but only one that mattered. And since there wasn't any way to know at the moment if he loved her more than he loved rodeo, there wasn't any point dwelling on it. So she pushed those thoughts away.

Searching the rumpled covers on the other side of Matt, Becca couldn't find Sarah. Alarm swept through her. Had the girl somehow gotten out of the suite? Becca checked the bathroom, then turned on a light in Hank and Alex's room. No Sarah.

Then she remembered Sarah's nap in Travis's room. She ran across the suite, thrust open Travis's door, then stopped with a hand over her rapidly beating heart.

Sarah lay on the opposite side of the bed, closest to a lamp Travis must've left on. It looked as if the girl had tried to slide beneath the covers but hadn't quite made it.

Becca shook her head and, with a relieved smile, walked around the bed to pick her up.

Sarah woke when Becca tugged at the covers. "H'lo, Becca."

"Hello, cricket." Becca had taken to using the nickname given Sarah by her father. The label seemed to fit the little girl, who was always hopping about and chirping endlessly. "I'm going to take you back to sleep with J.J. and Matt, okay?"

Sarah shook her head. "It's dark in there."

Becca sat on the edge of the mattress and pushed her hair off her face. "Are you afraid of the dark?"

"Sometimes." The girl yawned and

snuggled deeper into the covers, evidently intent on staying. "Will you tell me a story?"

Becca hesitated, then decided she could carry Sarah back to her room when she fell asleep. "What do you want to hear?"

Sarah patted the bed next to her. "Lie down, okay? I want to hear about the princess and the bull rider."

"I don't know that story." Becca started to stretch out beside Sarah, but the girl shook her head and tugged at the covers.

"No. Under here with me." When Becca settled between the sheets, Sarah turned to face her and sighed sleepily. "You sure you can't tell me the story about the princess and the bull rider? Unca Travis didn't finish it today."

Becca shook her head and settled her hand on the girl's shoulder. "It must be something your uncle made up."

The girl nodded. "I'll tell it to you. Okay?"

Becca chuckled, then tried to stifle her own yawn. "Okay."

"Once upon a time there lived a beautiful princess named Sarah, who lived in a beautiful castle with a beautiful white horse named Penelope. Sarah's father, King Hank, owned a beautiful magic bull named Lightning . . ."

Becca smiled at the story the girl told between yawns. Trust Travis to make up a fairy tale with a bull rider as a hero.

As Sarah's voice wound down, Becca's own heavy eyes drifted closed. Her last thought was that she hadn't even lasted until the princess got to the arena.

Travis stared at the door to Becca's bedroom. He'd intended to go straight to his own room. It was nearly two o'clock in the morning. But he hadn't taken three strides into the suite before he stopped. His entire body was strung as tight as a bull rope, ready to snap at the slightest pressure.

He'd spent the past three hours trying to think of an excuse — any excuse — to rush back here, to Becca. Now that he was here, he wanted to fling open her door, scoop her up and carry her away. Someplace where he could have her all to himself for the next three lifetimes.

He wanted to force her to admit she wanted him as much as he wanted her. Not only that she wanted him, that she needed him. Him, a rodeo cowboy. Then he wanted to bury himself inside her and hear her cry out with pleasure. He didn't care if they never came up for air.

With a muttered curse, he sailed his hat onto the long table and forced himself away from her door before he gave into the raging demands of his mind and body. As soon as he spun around, he halted abruptly.

Hank leaned against the wall just outside the kids' bedroom, arms folded across his chest, dressed only in jeans that had been zipped but not buttoned. A huge grin crinkled his face. "You remind me of myself, ten years ago. I don't know how many times I stood outside Alex's door at the Garden, wishing I had X-ray vision."

"I'm glad you find it amusing," Travis spat. "Why are you still up?"

Hank nodded at the kids' room. "Making sure cricket's still in bed. I found her in your room when we came in."

"I thought she'd grown out of wandering around in the middle of the night."

"So did we." Hank shrugged. "Probably all the excitement."

"Did Alex have a fit?"

Hank shook his head. "I slipped her back in her own bed before her momma found out."

Travis chuckled. "You old softy. Cricket's got you wrapped around every finger on her chubby little hands."

Hank didn't deny it. "I need to tell you something in case I don't see you in the morning. Jake called right after we came in. He found a doctor for Mrs. Larson. In Memphis, at the University of Tennessee Medical Center. She has an appointment on Tuesday. This guy specializes in 'untreatable' tumors like Mrs. Larson's. But even better — he has a ninety-percent success rate."

Relief tumbled through Travis, followed by a quick spear of hope. Maybe now Becca would admit she needed him. This was something he could do for her that she couldn't do for herself. A way to prove he was capable of hanging the moon in the sky every night. Would she turn to him for help? Or would she tell him again that it wasn't his problem? The possibility made him reluctant to tell her, though he knew he had to. They had to get Mrs. Larson to Memphis as soon as the Finals were over. There wasn't any time to lose.

If Becca refused his help, at least he'd know exactly where he stood.

"Did you tell Mrs. Larson?" Travis asked.

Hank shook his head. "Alex thought you should be the one."

"Thanks. I appreciate it." He unsnapped

his cuffs and pulled his shirt from his jeans.

"By the way, you're going to find a little surprise in your room. I thought I'd leave it there and let you decide how to deal with it."

Travis looked up. "What is it?"

"Go to bed. You'll see." Hank chuckled as he sauntered toward his room. "Sweet dreams."

After a puzzled glance at his brother, Travis ambled over and opened the door to his room. Half a step inside, he froze. He shook his head to clear it but when he looked again, she hadn't disappeared.

His heart thudded in his chest like jungle drums in an old Tarzan movie. Becca was in his bed, exactly where he'd dreamed of seeing her.

How? Why?

Sarah. Becca must've found Sarah in here before Hank and Alex got home, then fallen asleep after being bamboozled by his niece into climbing into bed to tell her a story. He'd fallen for that one — more than once.

Travis walked over and gazed down at the beautiful woman under his sheets. His entire body hardened as desire ripped through him. Several unblinking minutes passed as he brought his libido under control.

She was in his bed, true, but he couldn't keep her there. The entire family would know they spent the night together, and he wouldn't do that to her. He had to carry her back to her own room. Damn it.

But he didn't have to yet, did he? No one would know if he stole a few minutes of having her in his arms. He wouldn't wake her, just hold her. He might never have the chance again.

Yanking off his shirt and boots, he slipped between the sheets. As his arms wrapped around her, she murmured his name and rubbed her face against his chest with a sigh.

Travis thought his heart would explode. She wasn't shy about needing him in her sleep. Why couldn't she admit she needed him when she was awake?

With an uneven sigh, he tenderly kissed the top of her hair. As he did, a deep peace settled over him.

Just a few minutes, then he'd take her back to her own room.

He closed his eyes and let her scent saturate his senses.

Chapter Ten

Saturday, Go-Round #9

Becca awakened by slow degrees, aware only of a deep sense of comfort and peace. The slow thud of a heart close to her ear, the rise and fall of her pillow and the cocoon of warmth surrounding her evoked primal feelings of safety and belonging. Feelings she didn't want to let go of.

His scent was the first thing she detected, though her sleepy mind didn't immediately connect it to Travis. The warm, male odor was simply the smell of her mate, which she would've known had she been blindfolded in a room with a hundred men. Recognition made her smile and burrow deeper into his arms.

She fought reality as long as possible. When it finally hit, it came rushing in with the force of a flash flood.

Her eyes popped open, and she looked down the length of the long, strong arm connected to the shoulder she lay on. Her back was pressed so close to his chest, the only way she could tell where he ended and she began was the thin barrier of her T-shirt. His chin rested on her head, his warm breath stirring the curls. He'd worked his free hand under her shirt. It rested on her stomach, his thumb touching the underside of her breast.

The sudden awareness of his touch made the point tighten instinctively, and she smothered a groan.

How the heck had she ended up in Travis's bed? Did he have the gall to come into her room and —

Sarah.

A glance at crumpled covers across the bed told Becca the treacherous little girl had deserted her. How long ago? She couldn't see the clock, which rested on the nightstand behind Travis, but the light from the windows let her know the morning was at least half over.

She had to get out of there. She didn't have any hope that her mother wasn't awake, but maybe she could convince her . . .

No one was going to believe she'd slept with Travis all night and nothing happened.

She could just imagine what the Edens were going to think. And she refused to even consider what Travis was going to say about finding her in his bed.

She had to get out now, before he woke. Then maybe she could convince him she'd left when Sarah did. That is, if Sarah wasn't around to verify it. All of the Eden kids were honest to a fault.

Slowly Becca guided Travis's hand from beneath her shirt. Biting off the sharp breath that escaped when his thumb dragged across one nipple, she carefully laid it on his hip, then raised her head only to find her hair caught under his arm.

She tugged the curls from beneath the bulge of his biceps, then cautiously eased away from him. Wouldn't you know she'd have practically the entire king-size bed to move across. Why couldn't he sleep in a double bed like a normal —

Suddenly she found herself flat on her back.

Travis rose over her, pinning her to the bed. "Where are you going?"

"Out of here," she told him hotly, miffed that he'd foiled her escape so easily.

He shook his head as if to clear the sleep away, then groaned. "Damn. I must've fallen asleep. I meant to carry you back to bed before —" He glanced at the windows, then groaned again. "Sorry."

"Sorry? That's all you've got to say? Your whole family is going to know I spent the night in here. They're going to think we —"

He lifted a brow. "They're going to think what?"

Her eyes narrowed. "You know what I mean."

He feigned an appalled expression. "Why, Miss Larson, I'm shocked. I'm not that type of cowboy."

"Very funny," she said, fighting against his strength. "Let me go."

He stretched out beside her, anchoring her to the mattress with one heavy leg across both of hers. "Not yet. What will a few more minutes matter? If we've been damned already, let's enjoy our damnation."

Becca tried to reason with him. "I don't belong in here, Travis. I —"

"The hell you don't." He tightened his hold, even though she'd stopped struggling. "This is exactly where you belong. You know it as well as I do."

"No, I don't. What's your family going to say? What's my mother going to say?"

"That now we have to get married?"

Becca went absolutely, perfectly still. "Is that why you did this? To force me to marry you?"

"Though God knows I wanted to bring you in here, I didn't," he told her patiently. "I found you in my bed."

Her chin lifted. Him pointing out the truth did nothing to help her pique. "Only because I fell asleep while Sarah was telling me your stupid story about the princess and the bull rider."

He nuzzled her neck. "Want to hear how it ends?"

"I have to go."

"Please stay." He lifted his head and gazed down at her. "I may never have another chance to have you in my bed."

Bleakness warred with hope in his eyes. The expression made Becca's heart contract, and her anger vanished as quickly as it had begun. Somehow, she'd never considered the possibility that her refusals hurt him. His ever-present smile and wry comments masked his feelings well. Usually she could see beyond the mask. That she hadn't been able to on this subject told her how blind she'd been to his feelings. That he'd stripped away the mask himself told her how strong his feelings were.

Did Travis love her?

Would it matter if he did? Her father had claimed to love her and her mother, but he still left them when it came time to rodeo. He loved rodeo more than he loved them. Becca had sworn she'd never play second fiddle to a bronc — or in this case, a bull.

But as she lay in Travis's arms, the satisfaction she'd always found in that vow couldn't compare to the pleasure of his warmth pressed against her. Was this the feeling that made her mother forgive her father time after time, even as he ruined their lives?

It must be. "How can I leave you when you look at me like that?"

Taking her hand from his grasp, she slipped her fingers back through his hair and dragged his lips down to hers.

With a sudden growl, Travis rolled on top of her and slanted his mouth across hers.

Becca's breath caught at his sudden passion, but it quickly ignited her own. She wrapped her arms around his neck and pulled him even closer, reveling in the strength pushing her into the mattress.

When his tongue sought entrance to her mouth, she gave access readily, mating with him in a meager imitation of the act they craved.

Heat spiraled through her brain, searing away rational thought, then diving down to form a hot whirlpool at the juncture of her thighs. Even through their jeans she could feel his desire, building, growing, pulsing against her.

Travis lifted her T-shirt and covered her breast with his large, warm hand. The scrape of calluses across the sensitive peaks contrasted sharply with the gentleness of his caress. But she didn't want gentle. She arched against him to strengthen the touch, moaning with the intensity of the pleasure, the boldness of her need.

A slow rumble of gratification echoed deep in Travis's chest, and he shifted until his mouth took the place of his hand. As his tongue and teeth tortured the wet, hot bead of her nipple, Becca's hips rose against his, trying to satisfy the throbbing ache. Then his deliberate torment moved to the other breast.

She dug her hand into his hair. "Travis!"

The sound of his name, cried out in passion, made Travis lift his head and gaze down at her. She lay across his arm, her eyes closed, her breathing ragged, her mouth slightly swollen from the violence of his kisses. Her wet pink nipples thrust toward him, begging for more of his touch.

With a deep groan, he pulled her T-shirt down, hiding those luscious mounds from his hungry eyes. He hadn't intended to drag her beneath him, but when she'd turned to him he hadn't been able to stop himself. He should've halted after a few kisses, but she was like quickfire in his arms, scorching him with her heat.

If she was so hot after just a few kisses, what was she going to be like when he could finally love her like he wanted?

Moaning with a deeper frustration than he'd ever known, he gathered her close and rolled them to their sides. He wouldn't consider the possibility that he might never have the chance. If he did, he'd take her right here, right now, without giving a damn who knew.

Breathing deep to cool the hot blood pounding through his veins, he smoothed the curls back from her face. "Becca darlin'? You okay?"

She opened her eyes, then squeezed them shut tight. Groaning, she buried her face in his neck. "How do you do that to me? When you touch me, I can't think about anything but touching you back."

Her words made his body tighten, urging him to bury himself deep inside her. "Don't say things like that. Not right now, or you'll find yourself sprawled naked beneath me in two seconds flat."

She trailed her hand across his chest. "You mean I have the same effect on you?"

He pushed his hips into hers. "Can't you feel your effect on me?"

She threw her head back over his arm and smiled at him crookedly. "Good. Then I'm not the only one who feels like throwing something through every dang window in this fancy suite."

"Or bashing in the nearest wall."

A shudder of desire ran the length of her body. "What are we going to do?"

"There's only one thing we can do, darlin', we have to —"

She quickly placed a finger over his mouth. "Don't say it. I'm so confused and frustrated I'll say yes, and I might regret it tomorrow."

He wanted to force the issue, to make her agree to accept him right this minute. "What's it going to take to convince you that I'll never give you anything to regret?"

Her brows met as she considered his question, then a faint smile smoothed the wrinkles. "You can knock Buster Carlson down and give me a good luck kiss tonight. Since I didn't win the last two nights, I've got to win these last two rounds or —"

She cut her words off abruptly, pressing her lips together tightly.

He wished she'd confide in him about the loan, but he couldn't force the issue or she might find out about him agreeing to buy the Circle E out from under her. He placed a solemn kiss on her lips. "I'll be there come hell or high water."

She raked her fingers tenderly through his morning beard. "Other than that, I guess time is the only way to prove you're quitting rodeo."

Travis rubbed his hand along the dip of her spine. Time. The one luxury they didn't have. Joy needed to see the doctor in Memphis as soon as possible. And the loan for the ranch was due in two weeks.

Becca might agree to let him help with her mother's expenses, but she'd never agree to accept his money to pay off the loan on the ranch — not unless they were married.

Thinking of Joy's condition reminded Travis of Hank's news. Now would be the perfect time to tell Becca about the doctor in Memphis. Getting her to agree to let him help her would take her one step closer to believing in him.

"You'd better let me go back to my

room," she said in a soft, miserable voice. "I'm going to have to face my mother sometime."

"In a minute, I have something to tell you."

She looked at him. "What?"

He searched her blue eyes, the pale color almost crystal with the remnants of passion. He saw no suspicion there, only a quiet expectancy. "Jake found a doctor for your mother. A specialist in Memphis. At the university medical center there. He only takes cases other doctors have said are untreatable, but his success rate is ninety percent."

Instead of clouding over, her eyes brightened. "Ninety percent? That's almost a sure thing."

He nodded. "Jake made an appointment for Tuesday. If you agree, the three of us will fly out of here on Monday."

Her gaze dropped from his, and he hurried on, determined to convince her. "I know you can't afford it. It doesn't matter. I can. I want to do this for you. Please let me."

Pain flashed across her heart-shaped face. "You want to do it for me, or for my mother?"

"For both of you." He lifted her chin

with a gentle finger. "But mostly for you."

"Travis, I —"

"What?" he prompted when she trailed off.

She swallowed hard. "I just want to know what you expect in return."

"Just your trust." He ran his thumb over the velvet of her cheek. "I want you to believe in me."

"Believe you can do what?"

"Anything," he said simply.

Tears sprang to her eyes. "I want to trust you. I've never wanted anything more in my life. But I —"

"Shh." He didn't want her to voice any doubts. "For now, just say you'll let me take you and your mother to Memphis. That's all I'm asking."

"What about Cocoa?"

"It looks like Hank's going to have an empty trailer going home. He can haul our horses back to Wyoming."

Her eyes plumbed the depths of his soul. He didn't flinch from her unrelenting study. He had nothing to hide.

Finally she squared her shoulders as if readying herself to take on the weight of the world. Even with that fortification, her voice was barely audible as she said, "Okay."

He felt as if he'd just won the biggest

jackpot in Vegas.

After a quick shower and shave, Travis emerged from his room to find Hank reading the paper as his kids watched Saturday morning cartoons.

His brother glanced up. "You look like a happy man this morning."

Travis returned his smile. "It's a beautiful day."

Hank glanced pointedly out the bank of windows, which showed storm clouds gathering over the mountains to the northeast, but Travis ignored him and walked to the table to pick through the remains of breakfast.

"You kids didn't leave me much to eat," he accused.

They apologized distractedly, their attentions never wavering from Bugs Bunny. Hank, however, folded his paper and approached.

Travis watched him warily as he bit a cold link sausage in half. He knew what was coming.

Hank didn't disappoint him.

"I'm just going to ask you one question," he said in a soft voice the kids couldn't hear. "You *are* planning on marrying her, aren't you?"

Travis picked up a piece of toast. "The minute she says yes."

"Why?"

Travis's eyes narrowed. "That's two questions."

Hank obviously didn't care. "Are you marrying her because you love her, or because you want the Circle E?"

Travis glared at his brother. "If you were any other man, I'd rip your head off for asking that question."

Hank wasn't intimidated. "I'm the only man who'd ask, because I'm the only one who knows you've wanted that ranch your whole life."

How could he give Hank the answer he wanted, when he wasn't a hundred percent certain himself?

He drew in a jagged breath, then turned to stare at the lightning striking the distant mountains. "I want her, Hank, like I've never wanted any other woman in my life. A week ago, I'd have done just about anything to get the deed to the Circle E. I wanted to live there alone, until I forgot what arena dirt smells like. Until people forgot the name of the Million-Dollar Cowboy. Until I found a woman who didn't want me because I'm a rodeo star. Now I can't stand the thought of living on

Yellow Jack Mountain without her." He looked at his brother. "Is that how you feel about Alex?"

"Why do you think I left the Garden ten years ago when you and Claire decided I needed to rodeo? It sure as hell wasn't because I wanted to be bashed by broncs. I couldn't bear to be at the Garden if Alex wasn't."

"So I'm in love with Becca?"

Hank slapped him on the back. "Only you can decide that. But it sounds to me like you're head-over-spurs. You sure she doesn't want you for your gold buckles?"

Travis's smile was crooked. "That's the only thing I am sure of. She definitely doesn't want a rodeo star. Now all I have to do is convince her —"

The sound of a door opening made him glance back. Mrs. Larson emerged from her room with a furtive look over her shoulder. When she spied him, she smiled and walked across the room. She held a garment carefully folded across her arm.

"Good morning, Travis, dear. You heading out for more special appearances?"

"Yes, ma'am."

"I guess this is as good a time as any to give you this." She flapped open an incredibly beautiful shirt. The bottom half was red with flames bursting into the white yoke. "I've been working on this all week. Just a little something to say thank you for all you've done for us."

Hank moved away from them as Travis took the shirt with a mixture of surprise and awe. "You made this for me?"

"I measured one of your shirts for the size. I hope it fits."

"If you don't mind a little indecent exposure, we'll see right now." At her nod, he jerked open the snaps of his blue-striped shirt and pulled it off. Then he pulled on the new one. The soft cotton caressed his skin. He rubbed his hands over the appliquéed flames. "Fits perfect. I don't know how to thank you."

"Now don't you go saying things like that. Becca told me about the doctor in Memphis." Joy's hands fluttered, and tears shone in the pale blue eyes surrounded by a web of fine wrinkles. "You're a good man, Travis Eden. I'm as proud of you as if you were my own."

Emotion choked Travis, and he drew the frail woman into his arms. "I love you, Mrs. Larson. You were there for me when my mother died. You're the one who raised me from a boy into a man. There's nothing I wouldn't do for you."

Joy held on to him tightly for a moment, then pulled away and patted his cheek. "I won't keep you. I know you've got things to do."

Travis smiled fondly down at the woman who was his mother in everything but name — and if he had his way she'd soon be that. "Is Becca dressed? I was hoping she could go with me today, keep me company while I smile at the fans."

Joy shook her head. "Becca's soaking in the whirlpool. Looked to me like she's got a powerful lot of thinking to do. You'd best just let her do it."

Travis tucked his new shirt into his jeans. "As long as she's thinking about me."

"Don't worry about that, dear." There was a definite gleam in her eye. "If I'm correct — and I do believe I am — you're the only thing on her mind."

Travis grinned. "I won't be back until it's time to go to the arena. Tell her I'll pick her up here."

"I'll sure tell her."

Halfway to the door, he stopped and turned. "And tell her she's the only thing on my mind, too."

"Becca!"

Becca glanced down from the clock that told her Travis was ten minutes late to see Sarah holding up her arms. With a smile, Becca lifted the girl.

Sarah ran her hands over the red flames shooting across the yoke of Becca's shirt. "You look beautiful."

"As beautiful as Princess Sarah?"

The girl giggled and nodded. "That means you hafta kiss the handsome bull rider when he rides the white bull for a hundred million seconds."

"Will eight seconds do?"

Travis's deep voice from the doorway made Becca spin around. "You're la—"

Her words cut off abruptly as she saw what he wore. It was an exact replica of the red and white shirt she wore. "Momma!"

He noticed her shirt a second later, and grinned. "Well, I'll be a bull moose. Aren't we the pair?"

"No." She set Sarah on the floor. The girl immediately ran off.

Joy stuck her head out of the bedroom. "What is it, dear?"

Becca planted her hands on her hips. "You know exactly what's the matter. I kept wondering why you insisted I wear this shirt today. We look —"

"Like a couple?" her mother asked innocently.

"Like two peas in a pod?" Travis supplied, twining an arm around Becca's waist.

"Like twins!" J.J. called from the couch.

Becca pushed away from Travis. "I was thinking more along the lines of ridiculous."

He captured one of her hands and brought it to his lips. "We look cute and you know it."

She glared at him, trying to ignore the sparks jumping up her arm from his mouth on her skin. "Were you in on this?"

He shook his head. "When your momma gave me this shirt this morning, she didn't say you had one exactly like it. But I have to say you look hot."

"Very funny."

He grinned. "You ready to go? We're late."

"Don't you think one of us should —"

"Don't you two look sweet," Alex exclaimed. She'd been dragged out of the bedroom by her daughter. "Sarah, run get my camera."

Becca stifled a groan. "We don't have time, Alex. Travis was late so we have to get to the arena."

"Oh, pish. You've got time for one little picture. See? Sarah's already found the camera." Alex lifted the small black box to her face. "Put your arms around her, Travis. Smile, Becca!"

Becca rolled her eyes. Even her mother was conspiring against her.

Chapter Eleven

Saturday, Go-Round #9

Becca clutched her ninth go-round buckle as the lights came up in the dance hall. Just one more round to go. A round she had to win, or she could kiss the Circle E goodbye.

Travis leaned down so his mouth was close to her ear. "You want to dance, or go on back to the hotel?"

She didn't even try to suppress the shiver his warm breath sent racing across her skin. He knew she wanted him. What was the point in hiding it? When she tried, he just pressed until he got the reaction he wanted. "I'm tired and sore. I'd rather go on back if it's all right with you."

He drew her a hairbreadth closer, a subtle acknowledgment of her passionate reaction to him. "Fine by me. This late in the Finals, everyone's ready to head on back to their beds."

He turned her off the dance floor.

"Damn. There's Glen Egan over by the bar. Can you give me ten more minutes? I promised Hank I'd talk to Glen about the heeling mare he's thinking about buying from us. I took her out on the road some this year."

"All right," she said. "I need to visit the ladies' room, anyway."

He squeezed her waist, then let her go. "I'll meet you by the door."

It took nearly the entire ten minutes just to reach the ladies' room because she was stopped several times by people wanting to congratulate her on her win tonight, or who wanted to tease her about her and Travis's shirts. One lady even wanted to know if her mother took orders.

Though she didn't want to admit it, Becca knew what had possessed her mother to create the look-alike shirts. Joy was as convinced as all the Edens were that she and Travis were going to get married. Even so, Becca wished her mother hadn't chosen a fire motif. Wearing the same shirt as Travis was bad enough. That they looked like they were about to go up in flames when they stood together was downright obscene.

She'd heard the shirts had been a topic of discussion on the ESPN broadcast tonight. According to Alex, one of the television reporters had actually interviewed her mother — live on national television.

Becca pressed cold water to her face when she finished washing her hands. The ESPN anchors must be getting desperate for conversation after so many nights of having to come up with something new to say.

"Becca?"

She glanced up to see Kim Jackson's face in the mirror. "Yes?"

"Travis sent me in to tell you he'll meet you out by his truck. He needed to show Glen something out there."

Becca's eyes narrowed. Kim and CherylAnn had been thick as thieves at the Finals. "Now what would be in Travis's truck that has anything to do with a heeling mare?"

The barrel racer shrugged. "Why're you asking me? I don't know."

Becca gave her a false smile. "Thanks, Kim."

"Fine, don't believe me. You can wait around here all night for all I care." She flounced several steps away, then paused long enough to say with an eyebrow arched, "But I saw CherylAnn following them."

Jealousy stabbed without warning. Becca felt an overwhelming urge to rush outside and drag the bottled blonde off her man.

She froze with a hand on the lever of the paper towel dispenser.

Her man? When did Travis become *her* man?

A sudden, blinding flash of clarity nearly brought her to her knees. Though she'd done her best to talk herself out of falling in love with the rodeo cowboy, she'd gone and done just that. He'd resolutely worked his way around, under and over her defenses and put his bridle on her heart.

Damn his thick, cowboy hide.

Becca tore off the paper towel and slowly dried her hands.

What was she going to do now? Should she tell him?

The thought of looking into his sky blue eyes and telling him she loved him made her lungs so tight it was difficult to pull in air. What would he say? Would he tell her he loved her, too?

Becca forced herself to be calm. In order to tell him anything, she had to find him — and possibly save him from Cheryl- Ann's clutches.

But why would Kim tell her CherylAnn was following Travis? Kim was Cheryl-

Ann's friend. The whole thing sounded like a trick to get Becca out of the way so CherylAnn could pounce on Travis.

Determined to find out what was going on and call a halt to whatever it was, Becca walked out of the ladies' room, then paused as she searched the crowded casino. No matter what Travis had said about people seeking their bed this late in the Finals, the casino was packed. She could look all night without finding him.

On the other hand, what else could she do? Since he wasn't outside the ladies' room, she wove her way through the crowd, searching for the flaming shirt. She finally arrived at the exit. After waiting several minutes, she pushed the glass doors open to see if he was waiting for her outside. He wasn't.

The only thing left to do was check his truck, which was just a few rows away in the well-lit lot. It was just on the other side of that black —

"Well, lookee here."

Wade's voice made Becca skid to a halt. Wade, Kevin and Chance walked out from between two vans. Her mind had been so engrossed with the possibility of running into CherylAnn that she hadn't given a thought to the three stooges.

Then an appalling realization struck — they'd been waiting for her. Kim had set her up, probably with CherylAnn's help. The barrel racers evidently knew these three cowboys were determined to "melt her icicles" and delivered her to them like a steak on a plate.

She didn't think they'd force themselves on her in the middle of the parking lot, but she wasn't waiting around to find out. Spinning on her heel, she sprinted back toward the Gold Coast. Before she'd taken three steps a strong hand clamped around her elbow, halting her retreat.

Becca whirled to glare at her captor. "Let go of me, Kevin Chapman."

"Where you goin', sweet thing?" Kevin's voice had a distinct slur. His breath made her fear that they'd all go up in flames if anyone in the state of Nevada lit a cigarette.

A hopeful glance toward the hotel door told her no smokers were around. This door wasn't the main one into the hotel, but there were usually a few people coming or going even at this hour.

"I'm trying to find Travis." She yanked at the hand holding her arm and jerked loose, but the drunk cowboys had surrounded her in a slowly tightening circle.

Every time she tried to dart between them, one of them blocked her path.

Wade grinned nastily. "Didn't old Trav tell you? He's busy with CherylAnn tonight. He wants us to take you back to your hotel."

"You're lying. He told me he'd meet me at the door. He'll be here any minute. If you cowboys know what's good for you, you'll let me go right now or he'll have your butts in a sling."

"Ohh, we're scared," Chance sneered.

"C'mon, baby," Kevin said in a cajoling voice that made her skin crawl. "All we want is for you to be a little friendly."

Though she still couldn't believe they would force her to do anything, Becca was getting worried. "How friendly?"

"Just a little kiss." Chance stepped forward and touched a flame that danced across her breast.

Becca slapped his hand away and backed up, running into Wade who slid his hand across her bottom. She twisted away from him and landed against Kevin.

There was only one thing left to do. Scream.

"Leave me alone, CherylAnn." Travis shoved his way through the crowded bar toward the door. "You've slowed me down enough. Becca's waiting for me."

The barrel racer grabbed his arm. "No, she's not. I told you, she left."

"I don't believe you." He jerked away from her, but when he arrived at the door there was no sign of Becca.

CherylAnn smirked as she wound her arm through his. "See? I told you. Come on, let's go have a drink. For old times' sake." She gave him her sexiest smile. "And maybe for new times' sake."

The touch that used to turn him on now made Travis feel sick. He quickly disentangled himself again. "Where is she?"

"How should I know where she is? Probably back at the ho—"

At that point, an older cowboy walked out the door and CherylAnn's words were cut off by a scream. Becca's scream — calling his name.

Two thoughts hit Travis simultaneously. The most important was that Becca needed him. Now.

The second was that CherylAnn had set them up.

"Damn you." Whirling away from the barrel racer's clutching hands, he shoved through the door only to come to a dead stop. Where was Becca?

"Travis! Help m—" Her voice was suddenly muffled, as if someone had clamped their hand over her mouth, then after a loud male curse, she called again.

His heart hammering with alarm, he ran into the parking lot. As soon as he cleared the first row of cars he saw her. She struggled against three men. Chance, Wade and Kevin.

He was going to kill them.

Kevin glanced up when Travis was ten yards away. "Uh-oh."

The bareback rider released a violently struggling Becca and hightailed it in the opposite direction.

That left Wade and Chance. Piece of cake.

"Travis! Oh, thank goodness!"

He wrenched Wade's arm off Becca. After smiling grimly into his fellow bull rider's stunned face, Travis buried his fist in it. Satisfaction surged through him as he felt the bone beneath the flat nose give.

"Travis, watch it!"

He ducked at Becca's warning, narrowly avoiding the blow Chance swung at him. An elbow in his partner's gut knocked the breath out of him, then an uppercut to his chin felled him.

He whirled in time to see Wade staggering around a dark van.

A second later, another cowboy came running. "What's going on?"

It was the man whose timely exit had allowed him to save Becca. Travis knew he should shake the man's hand. Instead he reached for Becca.

She flew into his arms. Burying her face in his chest, she wrapped her arms around his waist and held on tight. "Thank goodness you came."

He pulled her even closer, wishing he could draw her all the way inside himself.

"This guy's coming around," the older cowboy said from where he knelt beside Chance. "Are you two okay?"

Without loosening his hold one bit, Travis glared down at his team roping partner. "I'm fine. Becca, you okay?"

She nodded against him, but didn't ease her grip. His heart expanded so much he thought it might burst from his chest. She needed him. She'd been in trouble, and though she couldn't know he'd be able to hear, she'd called his name. When someone's in trouble, they call who they want most. Who they need most. Becca called him.

At that moment he knew he'd be hanging the moon for her every night of her life. There'd be no problem flying so high. Love gave him wings.

"What happened?" the cowboy asked.

Travis wrenched his mind back to the situation at hand. There'd be time later to convince Becca to marry him. "They were forcing their attentions on my fiancée."

Becca didn't protest his statement, which either meant she was more upset than she was admitting or that she'd accepted the inevitable.

"Do you want me to call the police?" the man asked, placing a restraining hand on Chance when he groaned. "I've got a cell phone in my truck."

"Becca?" When Travis tried to pull back enough so he could see her face, she complied reluctantly. Her eyes were wide and her breathing was a little faster than normal, but otherwise she looked all right. "Do you want to press charges against these three clowns?"

She shook her head vigorously. "Nothing happened. Not really. They just . . . pestered me. Please, let's go back to the hotel."

"You sure? There's something I haven't told you. Remember I said they wanted to melt your icicles? These three snakes were in on a bet to see who could do it first."

Becca glanced down at Chance, who'd sat up to glare at them. She shuddered. "I just want to forget it."

Her fear made Travis want to kick his partner so hard he'd land in the Pacific Ocean. "What the hell did you think you were doing?"

Chance wiped at the blood oozing from the cut on his chin. "Ah, hell. We was just having a little fun."

"Fun? I'll show you fun." Travis squatted and grabbed Chance by the front of his shirt. "Who's holding the money for the bet?"

"Rick Ivey."

"You tell Rick to deliver that money to Becca's room by the time she leaves for the final go-round in the morning."

Chance sputtered. "But —"

Travis lifted him a few inches off the ground. "Every dime. Becca won this bet. Not any of you losers. You got it?"

The cowboy glared at his partner. "I got it."

"And you can forget riding with me in the tenth round, you son of —"

"No!" Becca grabbed Travis's shoulders. "If you don't ride, people will ask questions."

Travis stood and wrapped his arm

around her waist. "So? I want them to know this sidewinder for what he is."

"Please, Travis." Her pale eyes were huge as they pleaded with him. "For me."

Part of his anger eased away and he drew a finger down her cheek. "For you, darlin', anything."

Travis shook hands with the cowboy who'd stopped to help. The man introduced himself, then told Travis he'd take care of Chance.

Becca thanked the older cowboy, then let Travis guide her to his truck. He lifted her into the passenger seat. "You sure you're all right?"

She nodded. "They just scared me, is all."

Since he hadn't drawn his hands back from her hips, he caressed the firm curves. "They scared me, too."

She gave him a brave smile and drew her hand along the stubble on his jaw. "Thanks for coming to my rescue. You always seem to be around when I need you."

His heart squeezed painfully. "I always will be." Though she was already looking at him, he placed a hand under her jaw to make damn sure she understood his next words. "We're getting married tomorrow night after the banquet."

To his surprise, she didn't flinch or turn away or argue with him. Instead she took a deep, uneven breath, then quietly said, "Okay."

Chapter Twelve

Sunday, Go-Round #10

Her wedding day.

Becca stared at the blue sky beyond the open curtains. It was nearly eight o'clock. She really should get up and get ready for the final go-round, which started at eleven-forty-five today instead of six-forty-five like the first nine go-rounds. There was a lot to do.

She'd been lying in bed for over an hour, but she still couldn't believe she was marrying Travis Eden.

One minute she was delirious with happiness. Tonight she'd be holding Travis all night — while they were actually awake. She got so hot thinking about all the places she wanted to kiss him she had to push the covers off.

The next minute her terrified mind would demand to know what had possessed her to say yes. Travis Eden was a rodeo cowboy, and ever since her father died, she'd believed rodeo cowboys were a life form just under fungi. Was she out of her mind?

She must be, because she loved him. She loved him for being the kind of man a frightened little girl could run to in the dark of night. She loved him for taking the time to make her mother smile. She loved him for giving them hope for the first time in years that her mother wouldn't die. She loved his deep, rumbling voice calling her monkey-face. She loved the way he tasted and smelled when he kissed her. She loved the way his hard muscles moved under her hands when she held him close.

She loved him for all the things he did, all the things he said, all the things he was.

Surely she could overlook the one thing she didn't like.

She'd better, because now that she'd agreed to be his wife, there was no way he was going to let her go. He'd told her so last night after he'd scooped her from her perch, climbed onto the passenger seat, then kissed her until her bones melted. The windows had been so fogged from their heaving breathing, he'd had to wipe them off before he could drive back to the hotel.

Only one thing bothered Becca. Why did he want to marry her?

Did he love her? He hadn't mentioned love, so she'd been reluctant to admit her feelings for him. But what else did she have to offer him?

She had her body, true, and he definitely seemed to want that. But he could have practically any female body he wanted.

He had to love her, didn't he? Nothing else made sense. Maybe he was as shy about telling her as she was about telling him.

The thought made her smile. Travis shy? Right, and grizzlies were teddy bears.

With a sigh, Becca rolled slowly to a sitting position. Lying here wasn't solving anything or getting anything accomplished.

Rising, Becca showered and dressed. When she opened the door to the suite, it was empty. Seeing a note on the table next to a tray of covered breakfast dishes, she picked it up.

Becca, dear,

Don't worry about the wedding plans. Claire and Alex and I are taking care of everything this morning before the performance. Listen for a knock on the door, will you? The wedding dress you wore at the fashion show is going to be delivered before we leave for the arena.

Alex made the men take Travis out to the Whitehead ranch for a few hours. It's bad luck for a groom to see the bride the day of the wedding, you know. Travis went under protest, insisting he'll see you at the arena this morning and the banquet tonight. But I think Alex even has plans about that. The men took the kids with them.

We'll be back in time to take you to the arena at ten-thirty. Get some rest. You've got a big day ahead of you!

Momma

Becca smiled and folded the note. She'd awakened Joy the night before to tell her about her and Travis's plans. Travis had evidently told his own family. Becca was certain none of them were surprised. Alex probably already had a wedding chapel booked.

No backing out now.

Taking a deep breath to force away the panic, she returned to the bedroom. She had to keep busy for the next few hours or she'd be swinging from the balcony by the time they returned.

Fortunately there was a lot of packing to do.

Travis closed the door to the suite. He didn't have much time. Hank and the kids would return any minute. They thought he'd gone to his truck, but he had to see Becca, if just for a minute. He had to make sure he hadn't dreamed the love he saw in her eyes last night. He'd been worrying about it all morning.

The suite was quiet as he walked in. "Becca?"

"I'm here."

The soft words made him spin around to see her standing at the door to her bedroom. Their eyes locked and several heartbeats passed as they studied one another.

The uncertainty in her eyes alarmed him. He took half a step toward her, then stopped and held out his arms, willing her to come to him.

She took a hesitant step, then with a tiny cry, ran across the room.

Relief flooded through him. He wrapped her in his embrace and held on tight. His world tilted back up on its axis. Everything was okay as long as he had Becca in his sight. Everything was wonderful when he had her in his arms. "Let's go get married right now."

She chuckled and pulled back to look at him. "Alex would kill us."

"To hell with Alex," he growled, then covered her mouth with his. Familiar heat swamped his brain, and he deepened the kiss.

A few minutes later they came up for air. Breathing hard, her lips red and slightly swollen, Becca ran her fingers along his jaw. "The rodeo world would kill us. You're going to win your eighth bull riding championship today. All you have to do is stay on your bull for eight seconds and the gold buckle is yours."

"And you have to win the barrel racing championship."

Her gaze dropped from his. "Yes."

The bright edge of his happiness dulled. Her trust in him still wasn't complete. He wanted to make her confide in him about the loan, to tell her it didn't matter if she won the championship today or not, that he'd be paying Ote Duggan off next week.

But he couldn't tell her. Wouldn't unless it was absolutely necessary. He didn't want her to think he was marrying her for the ranch. He wasn't. He was marrying her because he couldn't live without her. He didn't give a damn where they lived, as long as she was there.

The realization amazed him, but he knew it was true. He no longer needed a house on Yellow Jack Mountain to make him whole.

With her sweet, warm kisses and loving heart, Becca had replaced the pieces of Travis Eden that were missing. He now knew exactly who he was and what he wanted to be the rest of his life — her man.

He leaned down and gave her a solemn kiss. "I've reserved a suite at the Flamingo Hilton. I want to be as far away from this family as possible on our wedding night."

The click of the door signaled his family's entrance. He turned them so his broad back was toward the door and gave her another quick kiss. "The hordes are descending."

"Travis Eden," Alex cried indignantly. "What are you doing here?"

He turned to see three irritated women standing in the doorway.

"Don't you know it's bad luck to see the bride before the wedding?" Claire demanded.

"Jake saw you before yours," he countered.

She waved his point away as Alex pulled

Becca from his arms. "Those were mitigating circumstances."

Travis frowned at Alex, but let Becca go. "And these aren't?"

Claire shook her head. "Becca has family around to keep her groom away. I didn't."

Travis pushed his hat back on his head. "I need to pack my things. Becca and I are not staying here tonight, and we're leaving for Memphis tomorrow."

"I'll pack for you," Joy offered. "You run along now. Everything's set for the wedding."

"Yeah." Claire came over and started pushing him toward the door. "You'll have Becca all to yourself soon enough."

He scowled at his sister. "Soon enough for who?"

Half an hour later Becca stood in the middle of her bedroom and ticked off in her mind the chores she'd accomplished. She'd packed all her clothes. The ones she was taking to Memphis were in a suitcase by the door, next to the overnight bag she'd take to the Flamingo Hilton tonight. The things she was leaving were ready to be carried down to Travis's truck tomorrow.

Alex would be following Hank back to

Wyoming in Travis's rig. When her mother was well enough to travel, Becca would fly home with Joy while Travis came back to Las Vegas to either drive her old truck home or sell it.

The wedding dress Becca had worn in the fashion show hung in the closet, delivered an hour —

"Becca?"

Her thoughts scattered, she glanced over to see her mother standing in the bathroom door. "Did you get Travis packed?"

"Not quite." Joy held up a slip of paper. "I wanted to give you this number. That banker in Riverton, Mr. Duggan, just called Travis. He said the papers for the Circle E were ready to sign. I didn't know you'd told Travis about the bank calling in the loan, so I just took the message."

Confusion made Becca frown. "I haven't told Travis anything about the loan."

"Do you think Hank said something? Does he know?"

Alarm flickered through Becca. "No one knows, except you and me."

Joy's brows furrowed. "What does this note mean, then? What papers is he talking about?"

Becca didn't want to voice the suspicion that popped into her head, thinking irrationally that if she didn't say it, it couldn't be true. But she couldn't stop her heart from racing with dread.

"Do you think —"

"What, Momma?" She was ready to believe anything other than what she was thinking.

Joy walked into the room and sat down on the edge of her bed. "Travis has wanted the Circle E ever since he was a little boy. Do you think he — No. Travis wouldn't do something like that to us. He was there when we lost the ranch the first time. Besides, he's marrying you."

Yes, he was planning on marrying her. Just a few hours earlier she'd been wondering why. Now with nausea threatening to make her faint, she suddenly knew. "What do you mean, he's wanted the ranch ever since he was a little boy?"

"Don't you remember, dear? When you were a little girl, you used to brag that you were going to marry Travis. He'd say he'd even marry a monkey-face if —" Joy's face went white "— if he could have the Circle E."

Becca sat down hard on her own bed, hoping her body would catch up with her heart, which had already plummeted. "He's marrying me to get the ranch."

She remembered Travis telling her about

the land he'd been trying to buy for ten years, but he hadn't said where that land was. She should've known it was the Circle E. It was the only ranch available close to the Garden. What she didn't understand was what prevented him from buying the ranch before they did. He certainly had enough money.

"So what are these papers of Mr. Duggan's?" Joy asked.

Becca stared at the piece of paper in her mother's hand. "I don't know. Except . . ." Suddenly, air refused to enter her body. "No. He couldn't be that low."

"What?"

Becca met her mother's frightened eyes. "I thought I saw him talking to Ote Duggan at the welcoming reception, but I wasn't sure. Then some cowboys started pestering me and I forgot about it. Mr. Duggan must've told Travis the land would be for sale if we couldn't pay off the loan. And they —" Becca swallowed the lump in her throat. "I saw them shake hands."

Joy's hands fluttered. "I can't believe it. Not Travis. He's helped us so much."

"What else could it be?" Becca asked, desperate for any other possibility.

"Are y'all ready to go to the arena?" Alex

pushed open their bedroom door after a brief knock. "Jake and Claire are here. They're going to take the kids and you two can ride with — What's wrong? Y'all are white as sheets."

"Nothing," Becca insisted, giving her mother a warning look. "Why don't you go on? We'll take our own truck."

"What? Why?"

Becca rose and faced the woman who'd treated her like a sister. Had Alex known about Travis's plan? Was that why the Edens had gone out of their way to draw her and her mother into their family circle? Pain like she'd never known before sliced through her. "Because we're leaving Las Vegas as soon as I ride out of the arena."

Alex blinked hard. "You can't. You're getting married."

Becca shook her head. "I'm not marrying anyone."

"You're walking out on Travis?" Alex asked, her temper clearly rising.

Becca squared her shoulders. "I'm not going to marry a man who only wants me for my land."

Alex planted her hands on her hips. "Sit your little butt right down. I'm going to hear this story from the beginning."

Becca didn't sit, but since she knew Alex

wouldn't let her go without an explanation, she stiffly recounted what they'd discovered. When Becca finished, she glared at Alex, daring her to deny it.

Alex didn't lose any time. "That can't be true. I know Travis loves you. I asked him myself if he wanted you because of the land. He's been trying to buy it ever since I've been at the Garden, but Sam Duggan wouldn't sell it to him because of something that happened years ago. Travis nearly choked me for even suggesting it."

Becca took the note from her mother's hand. "Then explain this."

Alex gave the paper a worried look. "I can't. Maybe Hank can."

"No, please, Alex, I don't want the entire family to . . ."

She trailed off because Alex was at the door calling her husband. When Hank came in, Alex told him everything.

"My brother is not a sidewinder. He'd never do something like that to you. He went through hell when you lost the Circle E. He wouldn't be the cause of you losing it again." Hank held out his hand. "But there's only one way to know. I'll call Ote right now and ask him what this is about."

Becca reluctantly gave Hank the

number. He went into Travis's room to make the call.

She sank onto the bed and put an arm around her mother.

Alex sat across from them and patted Becca's knee. "There's probably a very simple explanation. You'll see. Travis loves you. I'm as sure of that as I am my own name."

"He never said he loved me." Becca choked on the words.

Alex waved them away. "That's men for you, always leaving out important details. Hank did the same thing to me."

At that point, Claire stuck her head inside the door. "What's going on? Shouldn't Becca be getting to the arena?"

"Nothing is —"

Alex blithely cut Becca off and told Claire the entire story. Jake heard it, too, since he came in right behind his wife. At least he closed the door to keep the kids out.

Claire sat beside Alex. Even before Alex finished, Claire shook her head emphatically. "I don't believe it. Not Travis. He's —"

"Believe it."

The harsh, quiet words came from Hank, who now stood in the bathroom door. His face was grim, his eyes glittered with anger. "I'm going to kill my brother."

"What did Ote say?" Alex demanded.

"During their little talk at the welcoming reception, Travis agreed to buy the Circle E when Becca defaulted. Ote has the papers ready for Travis to sign."

Everyone in the room gasped except Becca. She could no longer breathe.

"But that doesn't mean he doesn't love her," Claire said. "If he could have the land anyway, why would he marry her if he didn't love her?"

"It's called hedging your bets," Jake said into the silence that followed his wife's question. "I don't know Travis very well but if he wants the land bad enough, it's possible he proposed in case Becca won enough money to pay off the loan."

Becca's back went ramrod straight. "I'm going to win that money. There's no way I'm going to let him have the Circle E now."

Alex shook her head. "I still can't believe it."

"What are you going to do?" Claire asked Becca after a silent moment.

Becca met each concerned gaze in the room. This family should've been hers. With one treacherous handshake, Travis had ripped them away. But the tremendous pain of losing the Eden family was nothing compared to losing the man she loved. She'd never hold Travis again. Never kiss him. Never hear him call her monkey-face.

Becca forced her lungs to pull in air. Maybe one day she'd feel like living again. Meanwhile, she had to make sure her mother did. "I don't want to see Travis again. Will one of you accept my buckle at the banquet? Whether I win or lose, mother and I will head for Memphis as soon as I ride out of the arena. I don't know how I'll pay for her operation now, but —"

"Yes, you do," Jake said firmly. "I'm on the board for a foundation that provides money for people who can't afford this kind of medical care. You'll have the money. Don't worry about it."

Becca tried to smile at him, though she was so numb she couldn't tell how well she succeeded. She suspected the money would come directly from Jake and Claire, but at the moment she didn't care that she was a charity case. She'd do anything to hang on to the small bit of family she had. She'd pay them back one day, even if she had to keep rodeoing. "Thank you."

Hank crumpled the paper in his hand and threw it in the trash. "Come on, we'd better get you to the arena. Don't worry about packing up your rig. We'll take care of getting your mare home."

Becca blinked back the tears stinging her eyes. "I don't know how I can ever repay you."

Alex reached across and hugged her close. "Just go win that buckle."

"That's right," Hank said. "We'll take care of Travis."

Chapter Thirteen

Sunday, Go-Round #10

Travis wasn't worried when he didn't see Becca at the temporary stables for contestants, although he did cuss his family for keeping her away from him. If the object of not letting the groom see the bride before the wedding was to frustrate the hell out of the groom, then whoever made the damn rule knew what they were doing. His brief taste of Becca that morning hadn't been nearly enough to satisfy him.

Buster Carlson adamantly refusing to let him by to give Becca a good-luck kiss didn't cause any alarm, either. Even when Buster told him Becca specifically asked him not to let Travis through. He just put it down to Alex and Claire's influence.

When Cocoa thundered out of the gate, Travis shouted encouragement. Becca ignored him, but even that didn't worry him. He knew she was concentrating on her final ride.

His heart sank when he watched Becca tip over the first barrel, but with concern, not worry.

He saw pain flash across Becca's face, but she gamely finished the course. There's no way she'd win the average now, which meant he had to tell her he knew about the loan on the Circle E because he'd have to pay it off. Damn. He was hoping she'd never have to find out about his moment of utter stupidity.

Tears streamed down Becca's face as she rode out the gate. She must've hit her knee again.

"Pull up on the ramp," he called as she passed him. "I'll be right out."

Laying his chaps across the back of the chute where the last bull he'd ever ride clanged against the bars, Travis waited until the next barrel racer had streaked past, then jumped down in the gateway. His left knee screamed a protest, but he ignored the old injury and ran out the back of the arena. Buster Carlson frowned at him, but didn't try to stop him.

Travis expected to find Becca waiting for him at the top of the incline that led up to ground level. She wasn't. Since he was the last bull rider up and she'd been the second barrel racer, he had plenty of time to find her and assure her she hadn't lost the Circle E.

He was a bit worried about what she'd say when he told her about his agreement with Ote Duggan, but believed she loved him enough to forgive him, especially now that it no longer mattered.

He walked along the dirt path winding around the rough stock pens to a large fenced lot that housed the temporary stable and contestants' horse trailers. When he cleared the first row of trailers, movement at the gate caught his eye. It was Becca's old truck pulling out of the lot.

She was leaving.

He stopped dead. No. It couldn't be. Why would she leave? Something to do with the wedding, maybe? Then why were Hank and Claire waving goodbye while Jake held Cocoa's reins? Why weren't they inside the arena, watching the action from their seats?

Something stank like week-old grizzly kill.

Determined to find out what, he stalked toward his family.

Hank was the first to see him. His

brother turned to glare at him, squaring his shoulders and planting his hands on his hips. Jake and Claire followed Hank's stony gaze, their own hardening.

Alarm bells clanged inside Travis's head. Why were they looking at him as if he were the grizzly?

He stopped several yards away. "Was that Becca leaving?"

"Of course she left," Claire said hotly. "What did you expect?"

Her vehemence took him aback. "I expected her to watch my last bull ride, for one thing. Where is she going? Back to the hotel?"

"After what you did to her?"

His sister was making as much sense as a sleepy two-year-old. "What I did to her? What the hell are you talking about?"

"Becca and Joy are headed to Memphis."

Hank's words hit Travis in the chest like a sledgehammer. "What did you say?"

"They're gone. For good."

"No." Travis shook his head. Becca wouldn't leave him. "We're getting married tonight."

"Fat chance," Claire spat.

Travis shoved his hat back and glanced incredulously between them. "What the hell is going on here? Why are you two treating me as if I were a skunk stinking up your house? Becca hasn't gone for good. She wouldn't leave Cocoa behind."

"Hank's hauling Cocoa back to Wyoming for Becca," Claire told him.

"Will someone please tell me what's going on?" Travis roared.

"Ote Duggan called today." Hank's voice was honed with a sharp edge of steel. "The papers for the Circle E are ready for your signature."

Travis felt as if a trapdoor had opened and his whole world had crashed through. "It's not what you think."

His brother crossed his arms over his chest. "Ote said you agreed to buy the Circle E when the Larsons defaulted. You saying that's not true?"

"Well, no. I did tell Ote I'd buy it, but —"

"Then get the hell out of my sight." Hank spat into the dirt at Travis's feet and turned away.

Travis turned to Claire. "Let me explain."

"You already did," Claire told him coldly, then she and Jake left, too.

Stunned, Travis watched his siblings walk away.

What had just happened? Had his family

actually turned against him? Without even hearing his side of the story?

What side? he asked himself grimly. He'd known as he was shaking Ote's hand what his family would think about the deal he was making. He just thought they'd never find out.

But there were extenuating circumstances. He couldn't let the Circle E be sold to someone else. Not when he'd wanted it for so long.

Did he want it enough to lose his family? Enough to lose the only woman he'd ever love?

No. It had never been that important, but he didn't know that until he'd found Becca again. Until he loved her. Until he knew she loved him.

Misery hammered through him, threatening his consciousness. He clenched his fists painfully to keep himself from keeling over. In the space of a few seconds, his whole life had crumbled into sand. He'd lost everything — his home, his family, his honor, his woman.

And it was his own damn fault.

He'd been so close to the life he'd been aching for. Love was within his grasp, and he blew it away with one stupid handshake.

What the hell was he going to do now? He couldn't go home to the Garden. His family couldn't stand the sight of him.

He laughed bitterly. He could buy the Circle E.

But he knew he wouldn't. He couldn't live on Yellow Jack Mountain without Becca. The whole point had been to regain the love he'd lost so long ago. Now love was out of his reach forever.

The only thing left to do was rodeo.

Feeling like a cartoon character whose chest had been blown away by a cannon ball, Travis turned back toward the arena. He had to make rodeo history.

After two steps, he stopped.

Like hell.

He wasn't going to let his life slip away this easily. He was going to make his family see that although he might be pretty damn stupid, he wasn't a stinking sidewinder. He'd been between a rock and a hard place when he made that agreement with Ote. Okay, he'd made the wrong decision, but he wasn't going to let them take away his home because of one dumb mistake.

He took two steps in the direction of the temporary stable where they were probably rubbing down Cocoa, then stopped.

No. First things first.

His family could wait. He had to go after Becca. He wasn't going to let her drive out of his life. He was going to catch up with her — run her off the road if he had to — and explain why he made that agreement with Ote Duggan whether she wanted to hear or not. He was going to make her admit she loved him, or make her look him in the eye when she told him she didn't. But he sure as hell wasn't going to let her go without a fight.

He hesitated, thinking of what the media and rodeo fans would say about him not showing up for his final ride. He'd be giving up a hell of a lot to go after her. How certain was he that she loved him?

Travis closed his eyes, took a deep breath and listened to his heart.

How certain was he? As certain as he was of his name.

Buoyed by newfound confidence, he dragged his keys out of his pocket and ran toward his truck.

Rodeo history be damned. He was more interested in making history of his own.

Becca leaned her head against the steering wheel and with a tremendous effort, held back sobs. She had no control over the tears, however. They'd been streaming down her face since she rode Cocoa out of the arena. She'd barely been able to see well enough to drive.

"A flat tire," she whispered. "I can't believe it. We're not even out of Las Vegas."

She'd been running on adrenaline ever since learning about Travis's betrayal. Now that the natural stimulant was gone, she was drained. She didn't even have the strength to breathe, much less change a tire.

"Is it bad, dear?" her mother asked softly, her hands fluttering.

"I don't know. Bad enough, I guess." Becca straightened away from the wheel. She had to find strength somewhere. The tire wasn't going to change itself.

"Let me help you," her mother offered.

"How many times have I changed a tire on this old truck? It won't take long since I don't have a trailer to unhook."

Joy reached across and dabbed a tissue against Becca's cheek. "Are you sure we're doing the right thing, dear?"

More hot tears burned her eyes, but she blinked them away. "What else could we do?"

"Give him a chance to explain?" she suggested.

Becca shook her head violently. "There is no explanation. Even Hank knew he was guilty."

"Still, I think you should —"

Becca yanked on the door latch. "I should change this tire, and that's what I'm going to do."

Travis eased his truck onto the shoulder of the highway and switched off the engine. He smiled faintly at finding Becca's old truck broken down on the side of the road. They'd come full circle.

She glanced up, frowned, then turned her attention back to the lug wrench in her hands. The glimpse showed him a face stained red and the early afternoon sun glinted off tear tracks on her cheeks.

At least she cared enough to cry. He just hoped she cared enough to give him the chance to explain.

Only one way to find out.

Taking a deep breath, he swung open the truck door and dropped to the pavement. Becca ignored him as he walked slowly toward her. He didn't see any sign of Joy. Since she didn't weigh enough to make a difference in the operation of the jack, she must be sitting in the truck.

Travis stopped right behind Becca who

knelt in the rocky sand, fighting to loosen a stubborn lug nut. He reached over her and added his power to the wrench. After a few seconds of effort, it gave.

"Thank you," she muttered.

"Move aside and let me finish," he said.

"No." She spun the lug wrench until the nut popped off.

Before she could fit the wrench onto another nut, he took it from her hand.

She didn't look at him. "I've been changing tires since I was eleven. I know what I'm doing."

Travis frowned down at the top of her hat. "Are you going to stand up and talk to me, or are you going to make me bend my stiff knee to come down to you?"

"Go away."

"No."

"Travis —"

"I never meant to hurt you, Becca."

Finally she stood, arrow straight, but didn't look at him. "No. You just wanted the Circle E. Well, now it's yours."

With a finger under her chin, Travis forced her eyes to his. "I'm not going to buy the Circle E out from under you. I never was."

She jerked her chin away. "That's not what Ote Duggan told Hank."

Travis placed his hands on his hips to keep from reaching for her. "Ote came at me during the welcoming reception, saying if I didn't buy it he was going to sell it to some foreign guys. I didn't want you to lose it again, but I sure as hell wasn't going to see it go to a damn foreigner."

"Then you were planning on buying it," she accused.

"Not unless there was absolutely no other option."

Becca studied his face for a long minute. The sadness he saw in her eyes made him want to drag her against him and kiss her until she forgot everything but his arms.

"So your 'other option' was asking me to marry you."

He shoved his hat back on his head. "Hell no. I felt so bad after I made that stupid agreement, I decided I was going to help you win the championship so you could pay off the loan yourself. So I talked to Harriet Bradley, then risked my neck to distract you. My original plan was to help you win the money to pay off the loan, then talk you into selling it to me for a profit. That was before I knew about your mother's condition."

"So that's when marriage came into the picture?" she asked pointedly. "When you knew you couldn't get the Circle E any other way?"

"No! Our getting married has nothing to do with the Circle E. I love you, Becca. Why can't you believe me?" Travis's voice cracked, and he lifted his hands helplessly. "I need you more than I need anything — including the Circle E. I don't care about the damn ranch anymore. I just want you with me every day, every night, every minute for the rest of my life."

She gasped softly but didn't say anything. She simply stared at him, assessing the truth of his words, clearly afraid to believe him.

He wanted to shake her until she saw the truth. But he knew that wouldn't work. All he had were words. "Why did you leave without letting me explain? I came after you to confess what I'd done, to tell you I'm going to pay off the rest of your loan, but you were already gone. Even my own family turned against me."

Her hands clenched at her sides. "Why are you doing this? You don't need me to get the Circle E. You can just —"

Becca stopped abruptly as a sudden realization hit her right between the eyes. She hadn't been on the side of the road ten minutes before Travis showed up. "What are you doing here? There's no way you could've ridden your bull before you left the arena."

His blue eyes delved into hers. "That's right. My chaps are still hanging on the side of the chute."

The implications of his action made her stagger against the truck. "You walked out on your eighth bull riding championship to come after me? It was practically a sure thing. All you had to do was stay on your bull for eight seconds, and you drew an easy bull to ride."

"Yep."

"Why?"

He tipped his hat back in frustration. "Because I love you, damn it. When are you going to believe that you're more important to me than anything else in this great big beautiful world?"

"You love me?" she asked breathlessly. "You really do?"

He threw his hands in the air. "Of course I love you. Why the hell do you think I asked you to marry me?"

"Because you wanted the Circle E."

He shook his head. "You just found out about my deal with Ote this morning. Before he called why did you think I was marrying you?"

She spread her hands. "I didn't know. You never said you love me."

He squinted at her. "You've never said you love me, either, but I know you do." After a brief pause, he pressed. "Don't you?"

"More than my life."

He took two steps and folded her into his arms. Becca closed her eyes and held on tight as relief surged through her, sweeping all doubt from her heart. Being in Travis's arms felt like coming home.

"Then how could you leave me?" he asked against her ear, his voice strained.

She pulled back and gazed up at him. "How could I marry a man I thought only wanted me for my land? Why did you make that agreement with Ote Duggan?"

He looked miserable. "Stupidity. Desperation. I've wanted the Circle E ever since you and your mother lost it fifteen years ago. Though it took me a while to figure this out, the land represented the love I lost when you drove out of my life that awful day. I didn't realize it until I found your love again. Once I knew you loved me, I no longer needed the ranch. If you want me to prove it, we'll let the loan go. We can buy another —"

She placed a finger over his warm, beautiful mouth. "No. Momma needs the Circle E."

His eyes searched hers. "You sound like you're going to let me pay off the loan."

His half hopeful, half fearful tone melted the last of her resistance. Uncertainty was a side of Travis Eden the world had never seen. He was always so cocky, so sure of himself and his abilities. That he was letting her see his raw need showed her how deeply he trusted her, how much he loved her. "Well, after all, it's going to be your home, too, isn't it?"

The joy that lit his face made an answering elation burgeon deep inside her. He swept off her hat and covered her lips with his.

Becca put every ounce of love she had for him into the kiss, making him groan as he pulled away a minute later.

"Damn it," he snarled. "We're in the middle of the highway. Why do you always kiss me like that when I can't do anything about it?"

She drew a finger along his jaw. "Save it for tonight, cowboy."

His eyes blazed. "Just wait."

A shudder of desire ran through her. "I didn't mean to make your family turn against you. It's just that they were there when Ote called."

"It was my fault, not yours. They'll forgive me, now that you have."

She glanced at the busted tire. "I guess we should fix this thing and get back to the arena. I don't suppose there's time for you to make that bull ride."

"Nope. And I don't give a damn. Let Grady win. He's been trying for eight years." He gave her a puzzled look. "Why are you grinning at me like that?"

"Don't you realize what you've done? By coming after me, you proved I'm more important to you than rodeo."

He squeezed her tight. "I've been trying to tell you that for days."

"I know," she said. "I'm sorry I didn't believe you. But I've had too many bad experiences with rodeo cowboys to believe one of you could give it up for good. I'm very happy to learn I was wrong."

He looked a little worried. "You know I'll have to attend rodeos to sell the stock. You'll have to go, too, since you'll be training barrel racers."

She nodded. "I don't care, as long as we're together. I love you, Travis. I'll love you as long as I live."

He smiled, his finger tenderly tracing the path of a tear. "I love you, too, monkey-face. I think I've loved you from the moment you were born. And I promise I'll be with you every night of your life to hang the moon out to shine."

When she gave him a questioning look, he smiled and dipped his head for another kiss. "It's a long story. Fortunately, I've got a long time to tell you."

Epilogue

One year later

"I'll see you tomorrow, Momma," Becca said into the cellular phone. "Take care. The snow's really coming down."

"I'll be fine, dear," Joy said on the other end of the line. "This old house is tight as a drum since Travis spent all that money on it. And he made sure I have plenty of wood."

"I love you."

"I love you, too. Happy anniversary. Enjoy your new home."

Becca's smile deepened. "I already am. Bye."

She pushed the End button and placed the phone on the floor beside her. As she did, strong arms pulled her back against a broad chest.

Travis nuzzled the hair away from her ear. "Momma's all right?"

They lay on a pallet of pillows and thick

down comforters in front of the stone fireplace in their partly finished home. For their anniversary, Travis had surprised her by bringing her here to a champagne dinner they had yet to consume.

"She's fine," Becca said as the now familiar ache of desire for her husband spread through her veins like spiced wine. "You know, don't you, that she'll never move in here with us. Not even when you get the upstairs finished and we actually get some furniture."

Travis raised up on one elbow and looked down at her. "Why not? There's plenty of room."

Becca ran her hand up her husband's strong arm. If the past year was any indication, she'd never get enough of touching him. "She says she was born in that old ranch house, and she wants to die there."

His blue eyes narrowed. "The doctor said she had another thirty or forty years left after her operation."

"I didn't mean to imply she was going to die anytime soon. She thinks we should be alone to have our family. She says she's just half a mile away, plenty close for her grandkids to visit her."

His frown stayed in place as he ran a finger across her cheek. "She doesn't have any grandkids yet. I just don't like to think of her alone."

"She has lots to do now that orders are pouring in for the custom shirts she makes. In fact, she's thinking about hiring some help. Besides —" Becca smiled in anticipation "— I have some news in the grandkids department."

Travis bolted upright. "You're pregnant?"

Her grin widened at the joy on his face. "Yep. I took a pregnancy test this morning."

He threw the covers back, then ran his hands over her naked stomach and slightly swollen breasts. "I can't believe I missed the signs. I must've been more distracted than I realized, what with Hank gone to the Finals and trying to finish this place in time for tonight." He met her eyes, his own full of wonder. "When?"

"I have an appointment with the doctor on Thursday. She'll give me an exact date. But I figure sometime around the middle of August."

Travis looked thoughtful a moment, then his handsome face broke into his million-dollar smile. "Then he was probably conceived in this very spot. Remember?"

"Why are you assuming it's a boy?"

"You have to admit the chances are good. The Edens seem to breed males. Hank and Alex have three boys now since Luke was born. Even Claire had a boy. Out of five Eden kids, Sarah is the only girl."

Becca sighed in defeat. "I was hoping to have a little girl for Momma to dress up."

Travis's eyes sparkled as he slowly leaned toward her. "Don't worry. We won't give up until we have a girl."

"I don't know about that. After about ten sons I'm sure I'll —"

Her protest was cut off by his lips, and soon she was lost in a haze of passion as Travis thanked her every way he could for her wonderful surprise.

Later, they lay spoon fashion, sated, watching the snow swirl against the wall of fourteen-foot-high windows looking south off Yellow Jack Mountain.

Becca burrowed against the warmth of her husband and breathed deeply of his musky scent.

"You're falling down on the job," she murmured with a smile.

"What do you mean?" Travis asked. "You were begging me to finish."

She pointed lazily at the windows. "You forgot to hang the moon tonight."

He chuckled and ran his hand across her

still-flat stomach. “Oh, it’s there, darlin’. You just can’t see it yet.”

Becca placed her hand over his and turned her head. She could barely make out his features in the dying firelight. “You’ve given me so much during the past year. Thank you.”

He searched her face, then placed a solemn kiss on her lips. “Stick around, monkey-face. The best is yet to come.”

The employees of Thorndike Press hope you have enjoyed this Large Print book. All our Large Print titles are designed for easy reading, and all our books are made to last. Other Thorndike Press Large Print books are available at your library, through selected bookstores, or directly from us.

For information about titles, please call:

(800) 257-5157

To share your comments, please write:

Publisher
Thorndike Press
P.O. Box 159
Thorndike, Maine 04986